ACKNOWLEDGEMENTS

I would like to thank everyone that has shown their support and encouraged me to continue writing. I would like to thank my three best friends; Brittany, Brittney, and Jackie. These girls have shown so much support for me. If it wasn't for them I might have given up on the book but they helped inspire me to continue writing. I would like to thank my mother; she has always supported me with anything I have chosen to do in life. Whether it be from art to writing she was always there for me, every step of the way. I would like to thank my grandmother who has urged me to continue doing what I do best and I would like to thank her for being there for me. I would like to thank everyone else in my family, and many other friends, who have supported me through this journey. Thank you. This book is dedicated to you.

The Story Continues...

Eshabel: Book Two

IMPRISONMENT
CHAPTER 1

Once again I found myself in the very chamber that held me prisoner before. The same shackles chaining me to the stone wall. The same pungent smell of decay burning in my nostrils.

I quickly noticed that the hole Estel blasted through the wall had been repaired.

This time there would be no one to rescue me. This time there would be no one to comfort me, no Reneir to save me from the Forgotten that entered the chamber. Now I would truly be alone. Now, it was up to me to free myself. To be my own hero.

Feeling along the back of my head my hand encountered a bruising knot that hurt if I applied any pressure upon it. I am lucky enough that my skull hadn't been cracked by the pommel of the king's sword. My head throbbed in pain.

I couldn't remain here, I needed to escape, to form a plan. My eyes glided around the room searching for an escape route. They landed upon the bared window. But then it dawned on me that I no longer had my staff, no magic to summon upon.

My eyes then fixed on the door. There was a possibility that one of the Forgotten held the key to my shackles. If the creature got close enough to me I could strangle it with a chain and steal the key away from it.

To my dismay, a Forgotten was not what entered the chamber. Instead it was the king himself.

"Finally awake I see."

"Unfortunately."

"You would do good to change that attitude of yours if you are to be my future queen."

"I'd sooner walk through the fiery gates of hell than be your queen." A snarl escaped me.

He did not seem too pleased with my response. "You would live a ravishing life style if you were to be my queen. All the riches you desire; I could give to you." He knelt before me, "And all I would ask for in return, is for you to give yourself to me. Every night." His hand reached toward my face. A smirk written upon his lips.

"Don't touch me. I would never give myself to you. I will never rule by your side, watching as you destroy and kill everything that dares defy you."

My cheek throbbed with pain once his fist came into contact with it. His knuckles cracked against my cheek bone. My vision wavered for a short second. "You think striking me would change my mind? You truly are a foolish man."

"Or maybe you are just a foolish girl."

"I would rather be labeled foolish than rule by your side."

The king left the chamber, slamming the door so hard behind him that the walls vibrated. He would return.

I needed to find a way out and soon.

*   *   *   *

I awoke laying upon the ground, my brain pounding against my skull. Looking around the small chamber I saw the ashy remains of the seal. The king had destroyed it. Despair washed over my being. We had failed.

Estel lay beside me, he still had yet to regain consciousness. Bracing my hand against the wall I rose from the ground. My body aching in protest, my legs shaking beneath me.

"Arendella?" I called out searching for my friend. She was nowhere to be found within the chamber.

Maybe she returned to the battle field to aid Hawke and Uthtor. But my eyes found her silver staff left behind on the ground. I fell to my knees beside it, grasping the cool silver in my hands. She never would have left this behind. Never. Andakile had taken her. Taken her from us. How could I allow this to happen?

At some point, Estel had finally awaken. Standing behind me his hand rested upon my shoulder. "We shall get her back Haimera."

I stood from the ground grasping Arendella's staff in my hands. "And we'll make that damned king regret ever stealing her from us."

*   *   *   *

Early the next morning a Forgotten entered into the chamber. When I heard its footsteps approaching the door I pretended that I was asleep. Steadily the creature walked toward me and once it was close enough I grabbed the chain that hung from my wrist and wrapped it around the creature's neck.

Shrieks that pierced my eardrums escaped from the creature, echoing around the room. I tightened the chain around the Forgotten's throat, crushing its windpipe. The creature fought back, it refused to die so easily. It threw itself backward crushing me against the stone wall but my grip on the chain didn't waver. Instead I pulled the chain harder until the creature's shrieks broke off as its body slipped onto the stone floor.

Before its body could melt away I quickly riffled through the pockets of its robe. Just as it was beginning to bubble I grasped something that felt like metal. Quickly I retracted my hand just as its body became that black tar.

What lay in the palm of my hand was not the key I was searching for but instead it was a silver coin. Frustration flickered inside of me. I tossed the damned coin across the chamber. The sound of it hitting the stone ground rang in my mind.

The chamber door was forced open and Andakile stepped into the room, chuckling. "I knew you would try something so foolish."

"Damn you to hell."

"I am getting *very* tired of that mouth of yours. I say it's about time I do something about it."

Without another word spoken the steel tip of his boot smashed into my ribcage. I felt one of my ribs snap in half. My breath was knocked out of me and I fell to the ground at his feet. Any sort of movement caused a wave of unbearable pain surging through my body.

"You can break my bones but you cannot break my spirit." I said through gasping breaths.

"We shall see about that."

He rolled me onto my back using his foot. Kneeling before me he made the mistake of getting too close to my face. Just barely lifting my head from the ground I spat in his face. A smile spread across my lips as his face contorted in disgust. Soon enough that smile was wiped from my face as he grabbed my left arm. Snapping the bones clean in two. A scream escaped from my throat as one of the bones broke free, ripping through my skin. Blood dripped down my arm and onto the stone floor.

"Ah, I do love hearing the sound of your screams Arendella." Grabbing a thin dagger from a notch on his belt he dangled the sharp object before my face. "If you won't willingly give yourself to me then I'll just take you myself."

The dagger traced down my face, my throat, and made its way down to my chest. The cool steel just barely grazing my skin. When the dagger came into contact with the fabric of my shirt the dagger ate away at it. Every thread that touched the sharp blade broke free.

No, this cannot be happening.

Dear gods please help me.

Panic began to wash over me as the fabric above my breast was being cut away from my body. The look on the king's face was that of hunger, a hunger for a pure girl. I would not give him the satisfaction. He might of broken my bones but not my spirit, not my will.

Then, something sparked inside of me. Like magic was hidden away, locked deep within the depths of my being. I focused on that spark, reaching out for it with my mind, grasping ahold of it and bringing it forth. My body thrummed with a surge of magic. My bones melding together once more. The magic had healed me and now I had the strength to break free.

Forcing myself to meet Adakile's gaze a smirk wrote itself upon my lips. The palm of my hand itched and burned as the magic clawed at my skin, waiting for me to summon it. Pressing my hand against the king's chest I looked him deep in the eyes, "Go to hell." My palm radiated a soft purple glow and a blast of magic sent Andakile flying across the chamber, his body slamming against the stone wall.

Quickly I made my way to the bared window, I pressed both of my hands against the cool metal and called upon my magic once more. The bars were blasted away from the stone and I finally had an escape.

A grunt behind me told me that the king was not dead. My body grew tired of all the magic I had summoned at once. And I needed what energy I did have left for the journey home.

One day I would bring him down. Sadly, today would not be that day.

Without risking a glance back I jumped from the window and landed in the lake. Memories flashed in my mind as I remembered what resided in this lake. Quickly I swam to shore and ran. I was free and I was going home.

Home.

Many days of travel passed by, the freezing winter weather almost claiming my life but my will to live urged me forward. I marched through snow that went up to my knees, marching through freezing air that nipped at my skin. Somewhere along my travel I had lost feeling in my fingers and toes. Maybe it was for the best that I lost feeling, I no longer would be aware of the pain my feet were in to the long walk home.

Finally my journey came to an end as I approached the grand gates that led into the wondrous kingdom. I fell to my knees as happiness and relief sparked inside of me. After so many days of travel I had finally made it, safely.

"I'm home."

INFORMING THE QUEEN

CHAPTER 2

"How could I allow this to happen? Why did I allow her to go to Menanor?" Queen Lyanthian sat upon her thrown, her head rested within her hands, weeping tears of sorrow. "I should have made her stay behind. I should have known this would happen."

We had to be the ones to inform her of Arendella's capture.

"You know as well as we do that she would never stay behind. She would of went, with or without your permission. She fights for her home, for us, and for you." Estel was right. But I knew that he too was feeling the same as Lyanthian. It was written upon his face, he blamed himself for her capture.

"We will return your daughter to you, I swear upon my life that we will bring her back safe and sound." Kneeling before the queen I placed my hand upon her shaking shoulder. Watching her grieve over her stolen child made my heart ache.

"I swear upon my life as well." Estel stepped beside me and lowered to the ground before the queen.

Suddenly a guard burst into the castle and rushed toward the queen, dropping on one knee before her. "Your majesty, we found Arendella laying upon the ground in front of the gates."

Quickly Lyanthian rose from her throne, "Bring her here, now."

As she said this another guard entered the room, carrying an unconscious Arendella in his arms. Her white-lilac hair was a tangled mess, her fingers a faint color of purple, her face was tinted red. Her lips a faint color of blue. The winter weather was cruel as it tried to claim her life.

She escaped and had traveled through the unforgiving winter weather, on foot. There was no telling how long it took for her to arrive at the gates, only to be claimed by exhaustion and unable to enter the kingdom.

Estel rushed over to the guard and took Arendella from his arms, he cradled her body close to his, trying to warm her with his own body heat. "I'll take her to her chambers, Haimera come with me. You'll need to change her clothes and bathe her."

I followed the elf up the stairs, down the hallway, and into her room. Estel kicked open the door that led into her bathing room and gently placed her body into the tub. Once I began to remove her tattered tunic Estel's face blushed a deep red and he left the room, shutting the door behind him.

After her clothes were removed I summoned upon steaming water for a bath. Gently I washed away the dirt that clung to her skin and brushed through the tangles in her hair. Once she was cleaned I summoned the water from the tub and began to dry her body. Then I slipped a sheer white night gown over her head and slipped the thin straps over her pale arms.

When she was fully clothed I called for Estel. The elf gently picked her up out of the bath and carried her to her bed. Placing her body down upon the soft mattress and wrapping her in silky sheets. He sat beside her, his hand caressing her rosy cheek as he stared into her face. His ocean blue eyes were drowning in concern.

A pang of pain bit through my heart, the pain clawing at the beating muscle as I watched him touch her. I wished to be the one in his place to be able to touch her in such an affectionate way, but I knew that wish would never be granted.

I knew that his heart belonged to her, and her heart belonged to him. It was foolish of me to be jealous, I knew her heart would never belong to me.

I had her friendship, and I should be grateful for that. Her friendship was good enough for me, at least in some sense I did have her love.

So, I left the room. Quietly shutting the door behind me.

* * * *

I awoke in my room to find Estel asleep in a chair beside my bed. He had moved the chair right next to the bed and his head rested upon the mattress as he slept. His hand tightly holding mine.

At first I believed this to be a dream or that I had found my own heaven.

Estel groaned as he moved to sit upright in the chair. His eyes fluttered open and a wave of ocean blue washed over me. A smile spread across his soft lips.

"I wish I could wake every morning to your beautiful face Arendella."

I tried to sit up on the bed but my body ached in protest as I moved my strained muscles. Reminding me of my escape from Raz'noak.

Estel saw me in pain and helped me to sit up, tucking a pillow behind my back.

"I was so worried about you, it drove my nearly insane thinking of what that king could be doing to you. Tell me, how did you escape?" He now sat upon the bed, still holding my hand in his.

I turned my gaze over to the balcony, the two glass doors were wide open, allowing the cool morning air to creep inside the room. "The king beat me, breaking one of my ribs and my arm. Then he took a dagger from his belt and began to chop away at my clothes."

Still avoiding the elf's gaze I continued, "I was determined to not let him win, not let him take away my virginity and then something inside of me sparked, like magic. I called it forth and used it to escape." Finally, I met his eyes, "The rest of the story you know, I was found by the gates nearly frozen to death."

"But we elves cannot summon upon magic without our staffs." His face was masked with disbelief.

"I know but what I tell you is the truth."

"I never doubted you, Arendella."

Changing the conversation to a much lighter subject I asked, "I do wonder who bathed me and changed my clothes." I raised one of my brows to the elf.

His face flustered a bright red, "I had Haimera to do all of that, I thought that would be the best decision."

"Speaking of Haimera, where is she?"

"She left after she bathed you."

Then there was a knocking upon my door and slowly it creaked open. Haimera popped her head into the room, "Seems as though I came at the perfect time." She smiled as she approached my bed, "I'm sorry to ask you to leave your bed but the queen wishes to speak with you in the throne room."

"What about?"

"She wants you to inform her of what happened during the battle at Menanor and what occurred during your imprisonment."

"Alright." I looked over to Estel, "Would you mind waiting outside? I will need her help to get dressed."

Estel stood from the bed and left the room, leaving Haimera and I alone. She smiled and walked over to the closet pulling out a light blue short sleeved dress. Then she came to my side and slipped off the night gown and pulled the blue dress over my head. Carefully pulling my arms through the short sleeves. Helping me stand from the bed she pulled the bottom portion of the dress down over my knees.

"Thank you, Haimera."

"You are more than welcome." She smiled sweetly and helped me walk toward the door, putting one of my arms around her shoulders.

When we left the room Estel followed us toward the throne room where Queen Lyanthian waited for us. Her Pegasus rose from the ground once it saw me enter into the room and glided toward me. She nudged her head against mine, I placed my forehead against hers, "I'm alright girl, no need to worry about me." I brushed my fingers through her soft mane, the hair was silky to the touch. Her wings folded around my body. The feathers caressing my skin.

When the queen rose from her throne and approached me, the Pegasus returned to its spot beside the throne. "I know that your body is exhausted but I must know about what occurred at Menanor and your imprisonment."

I gazed into Haimera's and Estel's eyes, we had failed the queen. Failed everyone. Sighing I returned my gaze to Lyanthian, "Andakile destroyed the seal. We have failed you."

"Now only two remain." She sighed, her gaze drifting down to the marble floor, disappointment flickered in her eyes. "Tell me of your imprisonment." She asked, not wanting to hear any more of our failure.

"He beat me when I refused his offer to be his queen. While he was beating me I felt some sort of magic spark inside of me, I called it forth and used it to escape."

Her eyes widened with shock but quickly the shock disappeared. "I'm sorry my child, I knew I should have made you stay behind." She completely ignored the part about me summoning magic that was impossible for us elves to do without our staffs.

"I never would have stayed behind. I fight for our home, Lyanthian."

"I know my child," She turned her back to me, "You may return to your chamber now and rest."

I felt as though she were hiding something from me but she would never do such a thing. Would she?

*　　　　*　　　　*　　　　*

Haimera helped escort me back to my room. Uthtor had summoned Estel to the barracks to discuss battle strategies. Though I may be Uthtor's second in command he suggested that I get some rest, allow my body to heal. So, Estel is taking my place for the time being.

Once I was seated upon my bed Haimera turned away and began to approach the door.

"Haimera, will you please keep me company?" I called out to her.

"Of course, Arendella." She smiled brightly and seated herself in the chair next to my bed, crossing her leg over the other. The slit in her dress's side exposed the pale skin of her leg. The emerald fabric complemented her eyes. There was a slit in the fabric between her breasts and the dress tied at the back of her neck, exposing her shoulders. She propped her elbow upon the arm of the chair and rested her chin upon the back of her hand. "What do you wish to speak about?"

"What happened after the seal was destroyed?"

She sighed, "Estel and I awoke upon the ground to find you missing. Many lives were lost. We journeyed back to Theleshara to inform the queen of what occurred, and that you were captured." A pained look crossed her face and she broke her gaze from mine, "I am truly sorry that we didn't come to your aid. We tried, Estel and I, but we had to return to Theleshara. We had to help the injured soldiers and take home the bodies of the ones we lost."

"I wouldn't want you to risk your life for mine."

A small chuckle escaped her, "Do you not know the meaning of friendship? Of love? I would be willing to lay down my life if it meant saving you. Estel would do the very same and we know that you would do the same for us."

My gaze wondered over to the windows, "And that is why I feared letting people get close me, they die."

"I won't ask of your past if it pains you but you shouldn't blame yourself for the death of others. Fate is cruel, and it decides when it is someone's time to leave this place." She reached over to the bed and held my hand in hers. "Allow yourself to love and to be loved without fear."

HIDING THE TRUTH
CHAPTER 3

"You know what she truly is. Why hide that from the girl?" Titiana stood before me with her arms crossed over her chest.

"You know why I must hide it away from her."

"Actually, I don't. Why don't you enlighten me as to why you hide the truth from her?" She placed one of her hands upon her hip as she waved her other hand within the air.

"You know how much power she possesses; how dangerous it could be if she ever summoned upon it."

"She already *has* Lyanthian. She has awakened the fae blood that courses through her veins. Allow me to teach her the ways of our magic."

"No. With the power of elves and the power of fae she holds a power that can destroy us all."

"So what are you going to do with the child? Lock her away forever? Continue to hide the truth from her?"

Titiana was growing furious with me. Her fiery hair began to glow and small embers fell from her fiery locks. Her wings twitched angrily behind her.

"Calm yourself Titiana. Even you know that her power is dangerous."

"Not if I were to teach her how to control it."

"My answer remains a no." I rose from my bed and stood before the two tall floor length windows, gazing out upon my kingdom. "Her mother's dying wish was for me to protect her. If it means that I must hide the truth from her in order to do so then I shall do it."

"You are making a mistake Lyanthian."

The fairy queen stood behind me, I could feel her eyes burning holes into my back as she glared upon me with anger. "Tell me, if King Andakile were to find out of her power what do you think he might do to the girl?" I asked her without facing her.

A sigh escaped the queen. "He would try to kill her to obtain her power. But you forget that she used her fae magic to free herself."

"He *will* kill her. He might not have known what sort of power that was, maybe he lost memory of what *exactly* happened."

"He won't kill her, not if I teach her the ways of my people's magic. I beg of you Lyanthian please allow me to do so." She pleaded to me.

"My answer remains the same."

"Her power could hold the key to ending these wars, putting an end to the king."

"No matter what you say my mind shall not be changed. Goodnight, Titiana."

Her light footsteps echoed throughout my room, "And do not go behind my back and try and teach her your magic. I shall remove you and your people from my kingdom if you do so. Your choice, Titiana."

The door slammed shut behind her as she stormed out of my room.

This was the right thing to do, to protect the girl from herself and from the king. She must never find out what she truly is and the power she possesses.

I glanced back into my chamber from the balcony. My words were harsh but this must be hidden from the girl, at least until she is ready to know the truth. I wondered back into my room and sat upon my small couch, next to it was an end table with a book laying across the top of it. In silver lettering the word *Elfara* was written across the aged old leather. I had traveled back to the hidden library and taken this book from it.

I plucked the faded red book from the stand and held it within my hands. For a while I only gazed upon the book, my eyes staring upon the one word on the cover. Slowly, I opened the small book and began skimming through the pages and yet I found myself at the very back of it looking upon the family trees and people said to be Elfara. A picture of a woman whom I used to know so well stared back at me, a line attached her picture to that of a man. A fae man. The line connected them as lovers.

A sigh escaped my lips as I shut the book and left my room to return it to the hidden library.

CONFRONTING THE KING
CHAPTER 4

"What the hell did I tell you?" Renier stormed into my castle, the gate doors slamming against the stone walls. A staff grasped tightly within his fist. Tarry liquid sprayed across his pale face.

"That you would kill me if I were to ever lay a hand on Arendella." I said as I rose from my throne with a smirk written across my face. "You also promised to rip my tongue out if I remember correctly."

Oh how fun this would prove to be.

"You broke your oath, now I shall kill you." His shouts filled the room as he charged at me brandishing his staff.

Too bad for him that he failed to notice my new found powers. Before the boy could even get close to me a force of magic blasted him across the room, his body slamming into the wall. He lay limp upon the ground.

"While you were hiding away from the battle at Menanor like a coward I was able to destroy another seal, gaining more power than the last time. You shall never kill me, all your efforts shall end in failure."

I kicked at his limp body forcing him to meet my gaze, "You were never truly freed from me, Renier. Queen Lyanthian might have rid my magic from your body but you shall always remain mine. From now until the end of time." He trembled beneath my boot.

"I do not care about what you do to me, beat me, curse me, kill me. I do not care. All I ask is that you leave her alone." The boy pleaded to me.

His pleas disgusted me.

Did he believe me to be a merciful king?

How foolish.

Then something occurred to me, I smiled as a plan seeded itself in my mind, taking root as it grew and manifested.

"Renier, pledge your undying loyalty to me and I shall give you something in return as long as you obey every command that I give you."

"If I pledge my loyalty to you, what will you give to me?"

A smile spread across my lips, "I shall crown you prince over the land of Lylanalian when I conquer it. Hell, I'll even give you your own kingdom to rule over. I shall capture Arendella and hand her over to you, you may wife her or do whatever you wish with her." I paused as his eyes widened, "But defy me again, or attack me and I shall make sure that you spend the rest of your pathetic life locked away in a dungeon. Then I'll make you watch as I take the life away from Arendella."

He believed every lie I fed to him.

I crouched over him, forcing him to meet my eyes, "Do I make myself clear?"

"Yes, your majesty."

So weak he was. So foolish and naive.

Growing tired of him and his foolishness I moved my foot off his chest. "Leave. Report back to me once you arrive to Theleshara." I dismissed him.

He left the castle without uttering a single word.

I had his complete and undying loyalty.

Never again would he dare go against me.

Once the boy was gone I made my way down into the dungeons. Descending down the staircase and making my way past the human filled cells, and came upon an old iron door. I pushed it open and my nostrils were assaulted with a foul odor. The large room was empty, save for a body length table resting in the center of the room. I approached the table and set to work creating more creatures for my army.

Using my magic I summoned upon enough tar to form the body of a Forgotten. The black mass pooled onto the table and I set to work morphing the liquid, forming the body. Once the shape was finished I drew a dagger from my belt and sliced my wrist. Black tar droplets spilled into the body. It began to bubble as my magic worked its way through the black liquid, a red glow radiated from it as life entered into the body. The creature's shrieks filled my eardrums as it took its first breath into this world.

"Hush my child, soon your hunger for blood shall be satisfied."

        *   *   *   *

Returning to Theleshara, I snuck back into my room. Calling forth my magic I entered into the open window and quietly shut it behind me. I pressed my forehead against the cool glass. The king's promise danced around in my mind. Arendella would truly be mine if he were to be king. Then I could keep her safe always, by my side she would stay. But in the back of my mind I knew this wrong. I knew helping the king was wrong. But I was doing it to protect Arendella. That reason should justify my actions, my betrayal, shouldn't it?

But if she were to find out then she shall never love me, she would grow to hate me and despise my existence. She would never speak with me again. She would join all of Theleshara in their chants and hisses of traitor while I burn. No matter how hard I tried to convince myself to stop helping the king something in my mind urged me to continue aiding him. Something seemed to whisper in my ears. Like a serpent's hisses rang in my eardrums. I shook my head vigorously trying to make that voice disperse. But still it silently whispered in the back of my mind.

The voice turned into multiple voices. They swarmed around within my mind like a tornado of torment. Their voices sang in agony. Crying out in pain. I clasped my hands over my ears and cried out wishing for the voices to stop.

"Get out of my mind!" My voice yelled out.

I fell to the ground, my body curling into a ball. I pleaded for this torment to stop. Wanting nothing more than to hear silence. But still the voices rang out in my mind until I finally forced myself to sleep.

RETURN TO ESHABEL
CHAPTER 5

Queen Titiana requested for Estel, Haimera, Renier, and I to meet her in the castle gardens. When I arrived I found Estel, Haimera, and the queen gathered around the frozen fountain but there was no sign of Renier.

    Snow piled upon the ground. The weather here has been strange as of late. One day it would be warm and the next snow fell from the sky like a storm. Snow crunched under my feet as I made my way toward the gathered people.

    "Ah, Arendella we have been waiting for you." Titiana peered over my shoulder seeming as though she were searching for someone, "Renier is not with you?"

    "I have not seen him since we traveled to Menanor."

    She appeared troubled by what I had said.

    "Then we shall do this without him."

    "If I may ask, what are we to do without him?" Haimera questioned the queen. Her arms wrapped around her shuddering body trying to keep warm.

    "My people are suffering. We have been away from Eshabel for far too long. Our magic is depleting and we are becoming weaker with each passing day. We need to return to our home." Her golden eyes were laced with sorrow as she thought of her suffering people.

    "But your kingdom is in ruin and you said it would take years for it to be rebuilt." I said to her.

    "Years for it to rebuild on its own. If you three accompany my people and I then we can restore my kingdom to its former glory. Please, I beg of you." Her gaze pleaded to us.

    I glanced over to Haimera and Estel, they nodded their approval. "Alright we shall accompany you. When shall we leave?"

    "At nightfall. I do not want Lyanthian to know of this, she has enough to worry about now. We don't need to add to the list of worries she has."

    *   *   *   *

It was time to leave Theleshara and journey to Eshabel. Haimera, Estel, and I snuck out of the castle. To make sure that we wouldn't be seen we tied a rope to the railing on my balcony and we descended down the rope, one at a time. Once our feet touched the snow blanketed ground we hurriedly made our way toward the gates where Queen Titiana and her people waited for us.

The queen silently greeted us as we made our way toward the crowd of faerie. I approached the massive silver gates and pressed my hand against them. My hand radiated a soft purple glow. I grew confused as I stared upon my glowing purple hand, usually the color was blue. Why was my hand radiating a different color?

Still the gates opened just as they always had so I pushed away that small worry and focused on our journey ahead. We journeyed deep into the night toward Eshabel.

Finally, we arrived at the golden gates. The last time Titiana and I traveled here there were vines growing along the gates with flowers blooming from the vines. The kingdom's seasons were spring and summer, allowing flowers and other plants to bloom year round.

Queen Titiana approached the gates, placing her dainty hand upon the gold. A soft glow radiated from her palm and the gates creaked open, allowing us to enter the kingdom.

We came upon the faerie's ruined cottage homes. Scattering across the ground in ashy debris. Titiana turned to face us, "Haimera would you please begin work here? Help the faeries rebuild their homes?"

"I shall do my best." Haimera approached one of the ruined homes, followed by a group of at least twenty fae, they dispersed and began to clean away the debris from the ruined homes. Cleaning the cobblestone streets.

I peered back over my shoulder to see Haimera chanting incantations. Debris flying through the air and landing into a pile upon the ground. Logs began to stack upon one another as they formed the first wall to one of the many cottage homes.

Next we came upon the kingdom's garden. Here was where they grew their food. Sadly, the garden had been trampled during the siege. "Estel, here I would like for you to help my people grow new crops. If you do not mind?"

"I would be more than happy to help." He bowed and walked toward the first row of trampled crops. It appeared as though corn had been grown there. He set to work calling upon his powers, making corn sprout from the ground.

A few groups of fae scattered across the many empty acres of land. The wee pixies fluttering throughout the air raining seeds upon the uprooted ground. Estel had much work to do here and Haimera as well, building new homes for the fair folk.

"Now, Arendella please follow me." Queen Titiana led me away from the garden.

I followed her through the kingdom and we approached a castle, her castle. The white marble structure was wrapped in vines, trees circled around the perimeter of the building.

"Come, child."

She pushed open the massive wooden doors to the castle and we entered into a vast room. Paintings of fae decorated the white marble walls. An emerald colored carpet stretched its way between massive pillars that led toward the queen's throne. It was not made of crystal like Lyanthian's but crafted from white wood. Leaf designs were carved intricately into the wood. The chair was covered with a green cushion for comfort when the queen sat upon it.

Once she was seated upon her throne she spoke, "Tell me Arendella, what did it feel like to call upon that power that aided in your escape from Andakile?" Her golden eyes narrowed as she watched me closely.

"It's hard to explain. All I can tell you is that when I began to think that all hope was lost something sparked inside of me. It felt like magic so I called it forth."

She leaned back in her chair, losing herself deep in thought. Her brow creasing causing her forehead to wrinkle.

"Have you ever met your father?" She asked not meeting my gaze.

"No. Not once."

"Did your mother tell you anything about him?"

"She never spoke of him. All I know is that my sister and I did not share the same father."

The queen was growing irritated, she rose from her throne, marching back and forth upon the marble flooring. Her wings twitched behind her back as if she were about to take flight.

"It angers me how much they have hidden from you, child."

"Who has hidden what from me?"

Titiana glided toward me, her hands gripping my shoulders forcing me to meet her golden gaze. "Queen Lyanthian has hidden much from you, masking the truth with lies."

I stepped away from the faerie queen, "She would never lie or hide things from me, never." I turned my back to the queen and began to exit the castle.

"Then why do you not ask her of your father? Ask her what that power was that you summoned. You and I both know that elves cannot summon magic without the aid of their staff."

"Goodbye, Queen Titiana."

She called out to me once more just as my foot stepped outside of the castle, "If she fails to give you answers then come to me child, and I shall explain everything."

*   *   *   *

As I was leaving the castle, a familiar looking fae man fluttered down from the sky and stood before me. His long green hair flowed along the wind, his bright green eyes glistened in the sunlight. Golden flecks seemed to dance around his irises. His cheekbones were set high and seemed as though they could cut through steel. He towered over me. Translucent emerald wings fluttered behind him, glittering specks fell from the wings and rode along the currents of the wind.

He bowed, "It is a pleasure to meet you again." He then stood once more meeting his gaze with mine. "My name is, Fiori. You were the first face I saw when I was born again."

"Ah, I remember now I gave you my cloak." I said as my memories flooded back to me. That was the day I was able to see *The Great Oak of Life*. "My name is, Arendella."

"I meant to return it to you but things got rather difficult." He chuckled.

"You may keep it I can have another one tailored." I smiled to him.

His wings fluttered with happiness, "Ah, that is so generous of you, Arendella! I shall treasure it always!"

He glanced over my shoulder, "Say, why are you leaving from the castle?"

I glanced back at the massive marble structure wrapped in vines. "The queen wished to speak with me."

As we were walking away the castle doors swung open. Both of us glanced back to see Titiana standing upon the stairs. Her fiery hair had a faint glow to it. Her wings were folded behind her back. As she descended down the stairs her pearly dress trailed behind her in a streak of shimmery fabric. She approached us with a faint smile upon her lips.

"Come, let us see the newly rebuilt Eshabel."

We entered into the town to see newly rebuilt homes for the fae. Cottages and shops lined along the stone streets. Newly sprouted flowers were scattered upon the ground, thanks to the help of magic this kingdom would no longer lay in ruin. Pixies danced within the air above us, their giggles filling our ears. Many of the fair folk reclaimed their homes and shops and set back to working on their regular lives. Though an air of despair still hung over the kingdom, the seal was still destroyed.

Then, Haimera and Estel approached us, seeming exhausted. They still carried smiles upon their faces because they knew they had helped these people and that was worth the exhaustion.

When they greeted us Fiori introduced himself to them. Bowing with a smile upon his face. "I thank you from the bottom of my heart for lending your help."

In turn, Estel bowed and Haimera curtsied to the fae man.

"Fiori has spoken for me." Titiana chuckled. "Now if you'll excuse me I must visit *The Great Oak of Life*." Her wings unfolded and she took off toward the forest.

When I turned to face the people before me once more I caught Fiori staring upon me. A smile spread across his thin lips. "What is it?" I asked.

"You're just a fascinating women, Arendella. Caring and very beautiful." He smiled brightly.

I felt my cheeks heat up. Estel then moved beside me, placing his hand on my lower back and pulling my body close to his. My body flared with heat at his touch. I glanced over at Haimera, her hand was covering her mouth as her shoulders shook.

"Oh, seems someone does not wish for me to compliment their woman." He raised an eyebrow to the elven man.

"B-But I'm not his woman. At least not in *that* sense." The words just tumbled out of my mouth in a fluster. My words only caused Estel to tighten his hold on me.

"I shall not intrude into your relationship." Then he turned to Estel, "You have a good woman there, don't let go of her because other men would love to have her." With that Fiori winked an emerald eye at us and took flight, disappearing into the sky.

Haimera broke out into musical laughter, tears glistened in her eyes as she giggled loudly.

"Oh my. You two are too adorable. Especially you, Estel, when you get jealous." She poked fun at him.

"I did not like the way he was speaking to Arendella."

"Mhm. You're still holding onto Arendella." She placed a hand on her hip and pointed to his arm around my waist and then smiled to us.

Estel cleared his throat, "I think it's time to leave."

Saying this he led me toward the gates, still holding me. Haimera trailed behind us giggling.

CONFRONTING THE QUEEN
CHAPTER 6

She sat upon her crystal throne, her sapphire dress spilling upon the marble flooring. The lacey fabric sat in waves upon the ground. Her golden hair styled in a fishtail braid that snaked over her shoulder and stopped before her ankles. Her hazel eyes examined me closely.

"Why did you wish to speak with me in private?"

"I have some questions that I *want* answers to."

Her golden eyebrow raised as she propped her elbow upon the arm of her throne. "And what would your questions be, child?"

"Tell me who my father is." I demanded to know.

"I never met your father nor do I know where he is. Your mother never spoke much about him." She sighed as she gazed over at her Pegasus. "When your mother came to live here she was pregnant with you, and your sister was twelve at the time. Your mother had left Theleshara and lived in the kingdom of fae for quite some time."

"She came back from Eshabel pregnant with me?"

The queen did not answer me, did not meet my gaze. She was hiding something; I could feel it. But what was there to hide?

"What are you hiding from me Lyanthian?"

She rose from her throne and turned her back to me as she began to leave the room. The sound of heels clicking against the marble echoed throughout the quiet room.

"Do not leave this room until you tell me the truth!" My voice rose in frustration as I called after the queen.

She halted, "You dare come here demanding answers from me, raising your voice to me. I have told you all I know."

"Lies. You know more than you say Lyanthian. Queen Titiana told me that you were hiding something from me and I won't leave until I find out what you are hiding."

"Then you shall leave here not knowing what you came here seeking to find."

With that, she left the room, her sapphire dress trailing behind her in waves of lace. Leaving me behind in the throne room left to wonder what she was keeping secret.

* * * *

The cool winter's breeze swept across my skin, sending a chill down my spine. Tendrils of white-lilac hair escaped from my braid and rode along the breeze. My eyes gazed upon the kingdom below me. A family of elves strode along the snow covered streets of the market. The children's laughter echoed throughout the night as they danced through the snow. The mother holding onto the father's arm, staring loving into one another's eyes. The smallest of the two children had fallen to the ground, the father rushed over to the child and picked her up carrying the child home holding her within his arms.

Loneliness enveloped my being, wrapping itself around my heart. I envied those children, they had both of their parents and their love. They were a family. I had lost mine. Never knowing what it was like to have a father's love. I wanted to know who my father was, needed to know. Someday I would find him, someday.

A warm arm snaked around my shoulders pulling my body close to another's. I leaned into the embrace knowing who it was. That familiar warmth surrounding me.

"Something troubles you Arendella." His voice was smooth and warm.

"All my life I have lived not knowing who my father is." I said to Estel, resting my head against his chest.

"Have you asked the queen about him?"

"I have. And I feel as though she is hiding something from me, she dances around my questions not giving me a true answer."

"She should not hide things from you that involve your life and family."

"I know, Queen Titiana told me that if Lyanthian did not give to me the answers I wanted then I could go to Titiana and she would tell me everything."

"Do you plan on going to her?"

"I do but I do not have the time now, Lyanthian needs us here for when the king decides to attack."

"Then go to her when the war is over. Take this chance to learn about your family. I never really knew mine."

Estel spoke of his family before years ago when we were children. "You knew your mother." I said to him.

"She left me upon the castle steps when I was only four years old. Every day as a child I hoped for her to return for me but she never did." He looked down upon me and the sadness within his eyes vanished and happiness flooded them. "If she hadn't of left me here then I never would have met you, Arendella. For that I am thankful."

I wrapped my arms around the elven man, pulling his body close to mine. I wanted to ease him of his pain and heartache. His arms tightened around me and he placed a tender kiss upon my head. I knew that since we were little he always questioned why his mother left him, if she ever loved him. I remember one day I had made a promise to find his mother for him, and I had planned to keep that promise.

"Estel, what if I do not live through the war? What if I never find out about my true family?"

His arms fell from my body, his hands now gripping my shoulders firmly. His ocean blue gaze locking with mine. "You shall live Arendella. If anything were to happen to you I could not forgive myself. Promise me that you shall live."

Estel's gaze pleaded to me with such sadness at the thought of my death.

My hand caressed the elf's cheek, reassuring him with my touch. "I promise, Estel."
His hand wrapped itself around mine, "I promise to live as well."

    *   *   *   *

  Later that evening, when Estel retired to his own chamber for the night, Haimera kept me company. She sat upon the end of my bed, her lavender dress spilling out in waves across the mattress and upon the marble floor. Her dainty fingers traced patterns along the bed sheets.

  "What did Queen Lyanthian and you speak about?" Her cat-like eyes gazed at me with curiosity.

  "I questioned her about my family, my father. Queen Titiana told me that she is hiding something from me." I pulled my knees to my chest, wrapping my arms around them and resting my chin upon them.

  "Did she tell you anything?"

  "Nothing." I sighed as I gazed out into the darkness of the night. "Haimera, do you know your parents?" The question was too personal, too intrusive but she answered anyways.

  She seemed to be lost within her own thoughts. She bit her bottom lip. "My father used to live here but left seeking a new life. He sailed across the Thelarian Ocean and found another land, a land occupied by humans. That is when he met my mother." A small chuckle escaped her as she spoke of her family. "He told me that she was the first woman he lay eyes upon when he stepped foot onto the land and that she was the most beautiful person he ever met. He said nothing could compare to her beauty. She had skin of porcelain and hair of ebony. Her eyes were as green as emeralds." As she spoke I pictured her mother. I now knew, which of her parents Haimera favored. "I wish I could have met her." She smiled but her brows creased with sorrow and her eyes glittered with tears.

  "What happened to her?"

  "She died giving birth to me." Her voice cracked.

  My heart ached for Haimera. The sorrow she felt. I knew she blamed herself for her mother's death. I reached my hand out and grasped hers. Her eyes stared upon our clasped hands.

  "After her passing my father returned to the land of Lylanalian but not to this kingdom. We went to the kingdom of Raz'noak because at the time it was ruled by humans. And there I lived until I was ten, my father wanted to live alone so after my tenth birthday we left. Until I was eighteen we lived in the forest outside of Cyfaserin until one morning I woke and he was gone, left me behind with only a note with the word sorry written across the paper." Tears glistened on her rosy cheeks as she reached into a small pocket in her dress. Within her hand she held an aged piece of parchment with a single word written across it. "I knew that it pained him to look at me because I reminded him so much of my mother. To this day I still do not know where he is." All these years she had kept the last word her father ever said to her. All these years she's lived blaming herself for the death of her mother and the pain of her father.

  My arms wrapped around Haimera, holding her in a tight embrace. My own heart felt like it shattered listening to her story. Being abandoned by someone you love is damaging, emotionally and mentally. She cried into my shoulder, her hot tears landing upon my skin. Her body shook and I held her tighter. There were no words I could to say to comfort her so I allowed my embrace to speak for me. Letting her know that I was here for her and I would never abandon her.

ESTEL'S PAST
CHAPTER 7

As I spoke to Arendella of my mother I couldn't help but remember the pain I've felt all these years. Was it really so easy for my mother to leave me? Did she ever truly love me? It couldn't be so easy for a mother to just abandon her child if she loved them.

*   *   *   *

"Mommy, where are we going?"
My mother tugged on my arm as she finished packing a bag of my clothing. We left our small house and wondered through the streets of Theleshara. The town was quiet, fast asleep in their land of dreams. Only the golden glow from the lanterns upon the homes and stores guided us through the dark of night. My mother's hold on my arm tightened.
"Mommy, please tell me where we are going!" I cried out to her as her nails dug into my skin.
She remained quiet, not speaking a single word. As I peered up at her back her shoulders seemed to tremble. Soon a massive castle was in sight. The queen's castle. My mother hurriedly approached it, dragging me along behind her. It was hard for me to keep up with her, my feet stumbled beneath me as I tried to run. We approached the marble stairs and my mother guided me up them. Finally, she faced me, kneeling before me and placing her hands upon my shoulders.
"Estel, my child, I cannot take care of you any longer. So I must leave you here, the queen shall take great care of you." Her lips shook as she spoke.

"Why can't you take care of me?" I questioned my mother.

She lowered her head and sighed, "You are too young to understand." Her eyes met with mine once again. Her delicate touch brushed my hair behind my ear. "Someday, we shall meet again."

She seated me down upon the first step and handed me the brown satchel filled with my clothing. She smiled, placed her hand upon my head, turned her back to me and she began to descend down the marble steps.

"Mommy!" I cried out for her as I stood.

"Be a good boy and listen to what I tell you." She stood at the bottom step not facing me. "Do not move from that step, not matter what do not follow me." The wind rustled her short blonde hair, her peasant dress swayed through the air. "One day, I promise we shall find each other again." With those parting words she made her way down the dimly lit cobblestone street and disappeared into the night.

Then the crystal doors behind me opened and a beautiful women stepped out of the castle. Her honey golden hair trailed along the ground as she approached me. "You must be Estel." Her kind voice spoke my name.

I nodded my head to the women. She was the elven queen. Her smile was warming as she stretched out her hand to me. "Come with me, child. I shall take care of you." Her hazel eyes were filled with such kindness and love.

I gathered my bag and placed my hand in the palm of hers. I rose from the step and began to follow the queen into the castle. My feet stopped at the threshold, I peered over my shoulder at the empty streets. My mother was gone. I turned my attention back to the queen who smiled kindly to me. As I entered the castle the crystal doors shut behind me.

*   *   *   *

Seventeen years ago my mother had promised that we would meet again. Seventeen years and she still hasn't found her way back into my life and maybe she never would. For all I knew she could be dead or somewhere across the Thelarian ocean.

Arendella wrapped her arms around me in a tight embrace. She knew the pain I felt. She wanted to be my comfort, and she was. Since we were children she has always been there for me. From the first day we met up till now she has never left my side. If my mother hadn't of left me upon the steps of the castle on that night, then I never would have met Arendella. Or maybe we would have, training as soldiers and going into battle together. Though, we would only be considered comrades and nothing more. She would be living in the castle while I lived in the town, gazing upon her beauty at festivals and never being allowed near her. Fate has a funny way of pulling people together and drawing them apart.

My arms tightened around the woman that stood before me. I would never allow fate to work its cruel hands against me again. This time I shall keep the people I love, I wouldn't allow fate to draw us apart from one another. Never again.

FORMING A PLAN
CHAPTER 8

"It seems to me that the king is targeting the smaller kingdoms first, working his way up to the larger ones." Uthtor stated as he gazed down upon the map that lay across the wooden oak table. Hawke, the black bearded dwarf, stood beside him, not uttering a single word.

His home was destroyed as well and he lost many people in the battle at Menanor. He returned with Uthtor to gather supplies and food for his people.

"You may be right. Now only two kingdoms remain, ours and Cyfaserin. Which one do you think he plans on attacking next?" Queen Lyanthian asked him.

"Cyfaserin. Their kingdom is smaller in size compared to ours." His finger pointing to the wolf kingdom that was sketched onto the parchment. "Though there is the matter of his kingdom." He said pointing to the far corner of the map. "Did it preserve a seal as well?"

"Cyfaserin is where you are to head to next. And as for his kingdom, yes it did preserve a seal. Though I know he has already destroyed it. That kingdom lay in ruin for almost ten years, that is until he found it."

He nodded his head and asked, "When would you like for us to depart?"

"You have only just returned to Theleshara. I am sure that you and your soldiers are exhausted but we also cannot waste any time." She pondered for a moment, "Three days. That is when you shall leave, that should be enough time for you to rest and gather whatever supplies you may need."

Uthtor nodded his head in agreement, rolling up the map he left the room, followed by Hawke, to begin gathering supplies. Now Estel, Haimera, Queen Lyanthian, and I remained in the room.

"What bothers me the most is that the king has not summoned his dragon into battle for quite some time." Estel stated.

"You are right. But he believes his army is strong enough without it. Though I fear that when the battle comes here, that is when we shall see the beast again." Queen Lyanthian answered him. "Though I did some research and found that there is one more dragon that resides in this land."

She turned her hazel gaze upon me, "Arendella this is a journey that I have been saving for you. The dragon resides in the kingdom of Cyfaserin but not within the gates. She hides away deep within the forest in her mountain home."

"You would like for me to speak with this dragon? How do you know that she is not like the other?"

"Trust in me child. I would like for you to go on this journey alone."

"I do not approve of this." Estel's face contorted in disagreement.

"I agree with Estel." Haimera chimed in.

"I am sorry but I will need for you two to aid Uthtor when the battle brings itself to Cyfaserin."

Before Estel and Haimera could chime in their disagreement once more I stepped in, "Do not worry about me, Queen Lyanthian is right. Uthtor will need your help."

"So it does not bother you staying out of the coming battle?" Haimera questioned me with an ebony eyebrow raised.

"Dear gods it shall bother me but the journey the queen has for me is just as important."

"It seems as though we cannot change your minds." Estel said, defeated.

"Now my brave warriors go and rest, gather up your energy. Ready yourselves for the coming battle."

Queen Lyanthian dismissed us from the room.

*   *   *   *

I watched as the trio left the room, Arendella glanced back briefly before shutting the door behind her. Her blue gaze was written in concern, curiosity. There was a reason as to why I was sending her to meet the dragon; to keep her away from the coming battle, to keep her safe. I know it pained her, knowing that she won't be there to protect the ones she held close to her heart. But deep in my mind I knew she wouldn't stay away from the battle long.

The door opened once more and Uthtor entered the room. I noticed that Hawke was not accompanying him.

"Why did you return? Are you not preparing for the coming battle?" I questioned him as he approached the table.

"I know why you sent Arendella on that journey alone." He said to me. I know he valued her as one of his best warriors. And I knew he valued her like a daughter. "I wish to keep her safe as well, Lyanthian. But you know we need her."

"Her journey won't keep her away from the battle long. She'll join it soon enough."

"You fear many things. But I know your true fear is losing her." He always knew what I was thinking, feeling. He saw right through me like glass.

"You fear for the girl as well, Uthtor."

"Aye, I do. But I don't hide her away from battles or hide the truth from her." Unlike the rest of my people, he feared not of stating his true opinion and feelings on certain matters. My title as queen did not scare him like it did so many others.

"I do what I think is best. And if that means hiding things from her then I shall. She is *not* ready to know the truth about herself."

"There shall come day were she shall find out. And that day is approaching faster than you think."

I tore my gaze away from his. I knew he was right and deep inside my being I knew that day was coming. My heart ached, my hand clutched itself over my chest.

No matter how hard I tried to protect her I always failed.

LOVE
CHAPTER 9

When I awoke early the next morning I found Estel sound asleep in the chair once more. Since I have been back he has not left my side, not once. His light snores filled the silent room. Reaching my hand over to him I nudged his arm to wake him. He stirred awake, his eyes barely open as he gazed upon me.

"Come here, I know that chair is not comfortable to sleep in." I moved over and patted the empty spot for him to sleep on.

He didn't protest, he slid under the silky covers and pulled my body close to his. Resting my head upon his chest I counted his heartbeats, 1... 2... 3... Again and again I counted as the sound of it filled my ears. His chest rose and fell as his lungs filled with air as he breathed it in.

I had promised myself that I would not allow myself to feel love in a time of war that I could not allow my mind to be clouded with such things. But my heart simply could not resist it anymore, I craved him. Every inch of him. His touch, his smell, his love. I wanted it all. Though I knew it was selfish but love is a selfish thing, to want someone all to yourself, to be the only one to be called theirs. I loved him and I would not deny myself this simple pleasure any longer.

"Estel, I love you." I admitted, finally.

I moved from his chest as he sat up. His hand reaching for me, cupping around my face, his thumb rubbing against my cheek. "To hear you say that makes me happy. But you told me that you could not allow yourself to feel love in a time of war. So tell me what changed your mind?"

My hand wrapped itself around his and I gazed into his beautiful ocean blue eyes, "You changed my mind. I refuse to deny myself the pleasure of feeling and being loved."

"Arendella, I love you with all my heart."

Without another word spoken between us his lips met mine. Oh how I missed the taste of him, the feel of him. His lips melded with mine, our tongues dancing together. His kisses were filled with passion and yearning. The taste of him filled my mouth and my body craved more, so much more. I tugged at his tunic, wanting to feel his skin against mine. Briefly breaking the kiss, he removed his tunic, exposing his muscled chest. His hands slid up my night gown and pulled the sheer fabric over my head, tossing the dress upon the floor.

Gently he pushed my body down onto the bed and climbed on top of me, his lips kissed my neck. My body was thrumming with heat as his lips met my skin. His hands caressing my body. His eyes met with mine as his kisses stopped.

"Are you sure?"

"I am."

My hands tugged on his pants wanting to slide them off of his lean body. When his pants slid off, his body was pressed against mine, our bodies seeming to meld together. My legs snaked themselves around him. My fingernails clawed at his back, digging into his skin. No longer could I tell where my body began and where his ended.

On this day we became one.

Our bodies, our hearts, our souls.

*   *   *   *

Early the next morning I awoke to see Estel's sleeping face. The sun's early morning rays bathed him in a holy light, he looked like an angel sent by the gods themselves. My angel. My fingers brushed through his golden hair, brushing it away from his eyes. His arms tightened themselves around my naked body and he brought me closer to him. He buried his face in the nape of my neck, breathing in my scent. His fingers trailed along my spine, barely touching my skin. His touch was gentle, loving. The softness of his lips kissed my forehead. Then his ocean eyes stared into mine.

"How are you feeling?" Last night was the first time I had ever made love to someone. He was concerned that he might have hurt me.

"I am alright." My hand cupped around his cheek and I smiled to him. I was happy, truly happy. I was now one with the man I loved.

He propped himself up on his elbow as I lay on my back. He hovered over me, his fingers gently brushed my hair behind my ear. Then his hand trailed down my body and rested upon my stomach. "One day, I would like for you to be my wife. One day, I would like for you to be the mother of my children." His gaze glided down to my stomach and a smiled formed on his perfect lips. His fingers traced the shape of a heart upon my skin. He met my gaze once more, he grabbed my hand and held my ring finger. "I promise to place a ring upon this finger."

My heart beat with joy, it filled with love. We had promised each other forever. And that promise we would keep until the end of time.

TWO MORE DAYS
CHAPTER 10

Haimera would visit me throughout the day, and some in the evening when sleep would not come to her. There were only two days left until we were to go on our separate journeys. She feared that once we departed that we may not see one another again, though I reassured her many times, worry still consumed her.

Today she brought lunch with her when she entered my room. The silver tray held mini sandwiches and glasses of cool water. She seated herself on one side of the bed, directly across from me and placed the tray of food between us.

Hunger did not bother me, for I had eaten a rather filling breakfast of eggs, thin roasted slices of ham, and a glass of milk to wash it all down.

"Arendella, you seem... different. I cannot quite put my finger on it but something has changed about you." Haimera studied me with those cat-like emerald eyes of hers.

"I don't know what would be different about me." My face flustered as I tried to avoid the conversation.

"Though I did see Estel leaving your chamber this morning, seeming rather happy might I add." Her ebony eyebrow raised as a small smirk wrote itself upon her plump lips.

She knew. She figured it out.

"How was it?" She grinned.

There was no avoiding it now, "Amazing. Painful but amazing."

"The first time usually is dear."

"But I thought you preferred women?" I asked her confused.

"It took me losing my virginity to figure out that I was not interested in men. Though I had struggled with feelings about woman for quite some time before then."

"Have you found a woman for yourself yet?"

She stopped eating her sandwich and placed it down upon the tray. "I have one that I am interested in but she is in love with another." Sadness filled her emerald eyes. Such sadness that meant she truly loved this woman. My heart ached as I watched her sit there in sorrow.

I placed my hand on top of hers, she raised her eyes to meet mine. "You will find the woman that is meant for you, I promise you this."

She smiled, a sad kind of smile as she gazed at our hands together. "I feel as though she is meant for me. But she shall never love me, not in the way I wish for."

Her gaze peered out to the balcony. The glass doors had been left open allowing fresh air into the room. She watched as the first snowfall of the day fell from the sky. Snowflakes drifting along the wind.

Words had left me, I tried to form a sentence in my brain that could comfort her but nothing came to mind. Instead I embraced her. Hoping that the hug would comfort her in some way.

"I need to prepare for the coming battle." Haimera removed herself from my embrace and approached the wooden door. Her hand resting against the dark wood, her back facing me. "Arendella, you have a blessing in my life since the day I met you. Thank you."

With those parting words she left my chamber, the door quietly shutting behind her.

My heart ached watching her leave, hearing the door close behind her.

I couldn't help but wonder who the woman was that Haimera's heart yearned for.

    *   *   *   *

Later that evening, after dinner, Estel escorted me to my room.

"Will you join me tonight?" I questioned him as we stood before my door.

"Later, the queen and Uthtor have requested that I help them with preparations for our coming journeys." He placed a kiss upon my brow before disappearing down the dark hallway.

I stood before the door, my hand resting upon the cool metal of the doorknob. Before I entered into the room I heard the sound of footsteps approaching. I turned around expecting to see Estel, instead it was Renier retiring to his chamber for the night.

This was my first time seeing him since the battle at Menanor. And I found it rather odd that he ignored Queen Titiana's request for help.

I approached him just before he disappeared into his room, placing my hand upon the door keeping him from shutting it.

"We haven't spoken in some time. How are you, Renier?" I questioned him with curious eyes.

His gaze never met mine, "I'm fine. I heard of your imprisonment, I am sorry I could not help you." A hint of sadness flickered in his voice as he spoke.

"There's no need to be sorry, it was not your fault."

He seemed to flinch at my words.

"Why did you ignore Titana's request for help?"

"I was busy with Uthtor preparing for the coming battle."

Curiosity ate at me, "He seems to need your help a lot these days."

"Indeed." He tried to shut the door.

"Stop trying to avoid me Renier." My voice was demanding, "You seem to disappear quite a bit, tell me why."

"How I spend my free time is none of your concern. It seems to me that you have been using your free time well." He said with harshness.

I was taken back by what he had said, "And what does that mean?" Anger rose in my voice.

"You know *exactly* what I mean. You and the elf seem to be getting along *very* well."

"Do not dare speak of him or how I chose to spend my time. That is none of your concern."

Though he spoke with harshness I could sense he was hurt, to hear that Estel and I have become one must of hurt him. But I could not understand why the news would upset him. Unless...

"I apologize for taking my anger out on you."

"Why are you angry?"

His eyes finally met with mine and there in his gaze I found a broken heart.

"I am angry that I could not be the one to win your heart, Arendella."

With those words he forced the door shut. Locking himself in his chamber.

I returned to my own chamber, knowing that Renier wanted nothing more to do with me. I had changed into one of my night gowns, this time a more conservative one. The long sleeves kept my arms warm and the thick fabric that reached down to my feet helped keep my legs from freezing. I shut the doors that led out onto the balcony and lit a fire in the fireplace. Soon the room was pulsating with a warmness that surrounded my being. I seated myself on the plush carpet before the warm flames, losing myself deep in my own thoughts.

I began to think of Haimera and her yearning for someone that may never be hers, I thought of Renier, I thought of the journey that awaited me in the coming days. Worry clawed at my mind and heart as I thought of the war that my friends were going to fight, without me. How could I protect them if I'm not there? I could only pray that the gods would watch over my loved ones.

A pair of muscular arms wrapped themselves around me. A pair of moist lips trailed down my neck. Warm breath traced along my skin. My love has returned to me. I turned around to meet a pair of ocean blue eyes. The love I found in them washed over my being. My heart pounded with joy.

"I missed that beautiful face of yours, Arendella." Estel said with a smile written upon his lips. "Being away from you is torture, all I want is to be with you forever." His hand cupped around my cheek as he looked endearingly into my eyes.

"Once the king is dead then forever shall be ours." My hand placed itself on top of his.

"I wish I could join you on your journey." He said with sorrow. "Worry will consume me while we are apart."

"Do not worry about me, you need to focus on the battle before you. I need you to live."

"And I shall."

His lips met with mine in a kiss of passion. A kiss of a promise to stay alive, to live through the coming battles. A kiss of love. A kiss of forever. We would spend tonight together. Wrapped in one another's embrace. Tonight and tomorrow until we part and then we can be together, forever.

* * * *

My dearest Arendella,

I am sorry that I cannot be there when you wake. Uthtor requested that I help prepare his soldiers for tomorrow. I shall return for you tonight my love.

Sincerely, Estel

His letter only reminded me that today was the last day we could be together until we parted for our separate journeys. I held his letter close to my heart wishing that he was here. Instead of spending the day drowning in my sorrows I dressed and headed for Haimera's room. When I approached her door I had only knocked once before it swung open revealing a rather happy Haimera. She threw her arms around me in a tight embrace.

"I am so glad that you decided to visit me. Saves me the trip of walking to your room." She giggled happily as I followed her into the room.

"I figured you would like to spend our last day together."

My words had caused sorrow to lace her emerald eyes.

"You say that as if one or both us shall not live through the coming battles."

"You know that is not how I meant it."

"I know. I only wish that we had more time together or that we could at least fight together." She turned to me with a smile upon her lips, "We make a great team."

"Indeed we do." I returned the smile.

"Now, I figured we could go to the marketplace. I am in need of new dresses and I would say that you are as well." She smiled as she put on a thick purple coat.

"I would not say that I am in need of any."

"But you are saying that you would like some?"

"Perhaps." We laughed as we left the castle and walked toward the marketplace.

We returned to the same shop that we had purchased my birthday dress in, well not necessarily purchased more like given to us. We were greeted by the same elven woman with the same warming smile. As we looked around the shop we noticed that the dresses had been switched out for the winter time. Each dress was floor length with long sleeves.

"Oh, there's so many beautiful dresses!" Haimera squealed with excitement as she set to looking at each one.

An hour later Haimera approached me with an arm full of colorful dresses, "You have not picked out a dress?" She asked me.

"Not yet, though I do see that you have picked out plenty." I said gesturing to her arm full of dresses.

"One has to look amazing on the battle field." She said batting her eyelashes.

"Haimera, it worries me that you choose not to wear armor during battles."

"I find that my movements and flexibility are restrained when I wear armor. Wearing a simple dress keeps me light, and my movements are faster."

"Still, it worries me."

"Stop worrying so much before your forehead is creased with wrinkles." She said while she poked her slender finger at my forehead.

We approached the shopkeeper to pay for Haimera's dresses. Haimera put up a fuss about me not buying one.

"It makes me happy to see you both return to my shop." The shopkeeper smiled.

"You have such lovely dresses, it's hard to resist."

"Thank you Miss Haimera. My daughter and I work hard on each of these dresses."

"Well, you both make lovely dresses." Haimera smiled as she handed the shopkeeper a hand full of golden coin.

"Oh my. I simply couldn't accept this." The shopkeeper said flustered.

"Think of it as a gift for your hard work." Haimera smiled and grabbed her dresses from the counter and we left the store.

Once we were outside the shop Haimera exclaimed, "Oh my! I hadn't realized how late it had gotten!"

The sun was slowly sinking from the sky as the light of day faded away. "It is getting late and I still need to pack for tomorrow." I said with sorrow.

Once we were back to the castle we parted ways so that we may prepare for tomorrow. I watched as Haimera rushed down a marble hallway toward her room. Once her ebony hair had disappeared from sight I began to ascend the stairs toward my room. When I approached my door the smell of roses filled the air. I entered into my room to find a small table had been placed in the center of the room and resting upon the table was a small cake. Two wine glasses rested at either end of the table. A trail of white and red rose petals led to the table. Before I began to follow it an arm wrapped itself around my waist.

"I wanted our last night together to be special." Estel whispered into my ear. His hot breath tracing along my neck.

He escorted me toward the table and pulled a chair out for me to sit. Once I was seated he sat at the other end of the table and began to slice two pieces of cake. He placed one slice on a small silver plate and handed it to me. Then he filled our wine glasses with rich red wine.

"I made the cake myself, I hope that it pleases you."

Hearing this I took a bite of the cake and my taste buds exploded as the sweetness of the cake entered my mouth. Red velvet. "It's delicious!" I exclaimed happily.

He chuckled at my excitement, "It pleases me that you like it."

"Have you prepared for tomorrow?"

"Mostly." He said as he swished around the wine in his glass.

"We won't be apart for long, Estel. I promise." I said as I reached across the table to hold his hand.

He held my hand in his, squeezing it tightly with a sorrowful look upon his face. "Let's not speak of tomorrow. Tonight is about us." He said as he rose from his chair and approached me. Once I stood from my chair his arm snaked around my waist and his free hand held mine. Together we began to sway just like we did on my birthday. He spun me around and brought me back to him. Our movements were in synch with one another. My arms wrapped themselves around his neck and my fingers brushed through his blonde, silky hair.

His hands rested upon my hips. I stared into those ocean blue eyes, drowning in their beauty. His gaze was swimming in love. "Forever." I whispered.

"Forever."

He placed a tender kiss upon my lips.

My hands slid up his tunic, feeling his muscular chest. His fingers traced along my spine, sending a chill through my being. This was our last night together for some time and I wanted to remember him, the feel of him in the lonely days to come.

Slowly he slid the sleeves of my dress down my arms, tugging it until it fell into a pool of ruby by my feet. He removed his tunic as I unfastened his trousers. His arms wrapped around my body pulling me close to him, locking my lips in a passionate kiss. The taste of wine and red velvet filled my mouth as we kissed, sweet and drunk with love. His lips moved down along my neck, leaving a trail of kisses upon my skin. Each kiss sent a rush of heat through my being. A soft moan escaped my lips as we fell onto my bed tangled together. He crawled on top of me with hunger filling his eyes. My legs wrapped themselves around his body, pulling him closer to me. We seemed to meld together, our bodies becoming one. My fingers tangled themselves in his golden hair while my other hand clawed at his muscular back. A pleasurable moan escaped him.

We spent the rest of the night wrapped in one another's embrace.

PARTING WAYS
CHAPTER 11

A group of us were gathered by the gates early that morning. The cool winter's air greeting us as it swept through our group of gathered people. I stood before Uthtor whom was garbed in war armor ready for battle. Thousands of soldiers marched passed us toward the gates, their destination was Cyfaserin. The sound of heavy boots stomping along the cobblestone streets filled the empty air. My gazed then fixed itself upon the dwarf, Hawke, who stood beside Uthtor. He was not traveling to Cyfaserin along with the soldiers, he was to return to his home and help his people rebuild what had been destroyed in the battle. Soon two people took their places on either side of Uthtor; Haimera and Estel. They were prepared for battle; it was written within their eyes. They were determined to win. Though, I had my doubts. The king has only gotten stronger and I couldn't help but think he would win, again.

"Be careful and may the gods watch over you." Queen Lyanthian had joined us to say her farewells. It pained her to watch her adopted children march into battle, not knowing if they would return.

She turned to me with a sorrowful smile written upon her cherry lips. She placed a tender kiss upon my brow before turning her back on us and returning to her castle. She wasn't one for long goodbyes.

Uthtor approached me, "Good luck with the dragon but if it decides to try and kill you, be sure to kick its arse for me." He said jokingly before he wrapped me in his embrace.

"I will." I said returning the hug. I had always thought of him as a father. He sure as hell was protective like one. He then joined his soldiers by the gate, mounting onto his horse.

"Be safe, my love." Estel's hand cupped around my cheek as he stared sorrowfully into my eyes. He pulled my face close to his and placed a tender kiss upon my lips. We starred into each other's eyes as his thumb traced over my bottom lip. "I'll return for you." He turned his back to me and joined Uthtor by the gates, mounting onto his own horse.

Finally, it was Haimera's turn to say her goodbye. "Arendella, you are my dearest friend." She said as she took hold of one of my hands. "If you trust me, I ask you to close your eyes. Just for a moment." I looked upon her with confusion but I did as she asked. I felt her cold hand upon my cheek and then I felt the softness of her lips against mine. The kiss was brief but it held meaning. When my eyes were once again open, I gazed into her face. And then I knew that I was the woman that her heart yearned for. "I love you, Arendella." She said with a sorrowful kind of happiness. Happiness that she finally admitted her feelings but sorrow that she could never call me hers.

Without allowing me a chance to speak she turned around and rushed toward the gates, her ebony hair whipping through the air. Once she was mounted onto her horse Uthtor led his army toward Cyfaserin. When they were gone from sight I set off just behind them, though our destinations were Cyfaserin our paths were different. I had to travel through the forest to reach the home of the dragon. And so I traveled. Alone.

Night had fallen and it was difficult to see through the darkness of the night. Using my staff, I called upon a small ball of fire to guide my way with its light. I traveled through the dense forest, tripping over tree roots, and moving branches out of the way. Once in a while I would hear the rustle of leaves and the snapping of twigs as small creatures ran through the night. The howls of wolves echoed in the distance. And that's how I knew that I was close to Cyfaserin, the kingdom of wolven people. I pushed onward toward the dragon's cave home. Finding it would prove to be tricky, especially in the darkness of the night.

I remembered what Lyanthian had told me, *"Look for an opening into the mountain with the symbol of protection upon it. In order to enter you must leave all weapons behind or you shall not be allowed entrance in."*

After many hours of searching through the forest I came upon a clearing that exposed the side of the mountain. I searched along the rocky base of it until I found a rather large opening. Raising the ball of fire toward the top of the opening I found the symbol of protection carved into the stone. A circle with lines cutting across it in the shape of an X with triangles that pointed out from the ends of the lines. Resting my staff against the side of the mountain I unfastened my belt that held my daggers and the sheath that held my sword. I dropped the weapons next to my staff and entered into the home of the dragon.

What brings you into my home, elf? The dragon's voice echoed through my mind, its voice reminding me of a middle aged woman.

When I approached the dragon closer torches lit a flame along the mountain walls. The large beast stood before me, its scales as white as first winter's snow with eyes that glistened like brilliant sapphires.

"Queen Lyanthian has sent me here to request your aid."

The dragon kept watchful eyes upon me. Her gaze sliding down my being. *Why does she request my aid?*

"King Andakile has destroyed three of the seals and has acquired the aid of a dragon, much like yourself."

My brother, Thorodan. This is troubling news to hear. Now, only two seals remain. Which kingdom is he to destroy next?

"Cyfaserin."

The dragon growled with frustration and anger. *When was the last time my brother was seen in battle?*

"When the king destroyed the first seal in Eshabel. Months ago."

I cannot fight in a battle that my brother is not a part of, if he is not in the coming battle then I shall not be there to aid you. That is why my brother has not appeared in battle for quite some time.

"Why?" I asked angrily.

I am a dragon of peace. I do not wish to harm or bring death upon any living being. I do not wish to fight my own blood but I shall if it has to be done.

"Then I was sent here for nothing when I could have joined the soldiers in battle!"

Calm yourself elf. Your journey has a purpose. Lyanthian knew what my answer was to be. The dragon made herself eye-level with me. Her brilliant eyes staring into mine. *Hold out you hand.*

I did as she asked and stretched my hand out toward her, exposing my palm. The dragon closed her eyes and I felt a shift in the air as she called upon her magic. Water manifested with the air above my hand. It glowed brightly as it formed the shape of a small rock. The water hardened forming a small, clear crystal. Thin strands of twine wrapped around the crystal turning it into a necklace. The small crystal landed in the palm of my hand, it radiated a faint glow.

Use this to call upon my aid when my brother is in the fight. I am the only one who can stop him. I wish you luck in the battle to come, Arendella.

When the dragon addressed me by my name I was taken back. "How did you know my name?"

Before she could answer me her head snapped up and her eyes gazed toward the opening of the cave. *Go now child. For a battle awaits.*

Without hesitation I ran toward the entrance. Once I was out of the cave I fastened my belt around my waist once more and sheathed my sword. Grabbing my staff I began to rush through the forest, there were too many trees and it prevented me from bringing a horse into the forest along with me. So I had to run to Cyfaserin, on foot.

Sounds of battle echoed far off into the distance. The battle had begun. I feared I wouldn't be there in time. I feared that I would be too late to stop the king from destroying another seal. So much fear welled inside my being as the sounds of battle grew near. I urged my body forward, to run faster. My heart pounded rapidly within my chest. Soon my eyes landed upon the battle. Wolves sprang forth and attacked at the never ending horde of Forgotten. Snarls and yelps filled the air as the evil creatures stabbed at the wolves repeatedly until their bodies ceased to move. Corpses were scattered upon the ground. Elves, wolves, and people who were in mid transformation. Half of their bodies appeared to be human while the other half appeared to be wolf. The torso of a man had the legs and tail of a wolf.

Many of the Cyfasin people remained in their human forms to fight with swords and bows and arrows. The archers were placed at the watch platforms inside the gates firing arrows into the night sky. One arrow whizzed past my ear, almost nipping at my skin.

Grasping my staff within my hands I rushed into the battle in search of Estel and Haimera, in hopes that they were still alive and fighting together. The dagger end of my staff slashed through Forgotten as they dared stand in my way. The tar from their bodies sprayed across me. Coating me in that black liquid. I spotted a woman charging toward me, I knew she was Cyfasin. Though in human form they still had the ears and tail of a wolf. Her wavy blonde hair whipped through the air as she rushed toward me brandishing her sword.

"Get down!" She demanded.

Obeying her command I knelt to the earth and the woman leaped into the air and her sword slashed through the body of a Forgotten, cutting it clean in two. The woman then turned and faced me once more. Brown cloth bound her breast and a frayed skirt, with a slit in the fabric that reached up to her thigh, hung low at her waist. Red tribal tattoos inked the skin on her upper arms, wrapping around them. Her blonde hair fell in waves down to her waist with several small braids scattered throughout her blonde locks. "You are Arendella I presume?" Her ears flickered.

"Yes, now you get down." She did as I said and I sliced the head off of one Forgotten.

Deciding that facing each other while speaking was not the safest thing to do so we fought back to back as we spoke. "And I presume you are Crescent?"

"The one and only." She laughed as her sword bit through the heart of a Forgotten

"Where is your father, Lone Claw?"

"Fighting somewhere on the battle field alongside an elf named Uthtor."

I summoned upon my magic, calling forth lighting that thundered from the crystal atop my staff. It rained from the sky killing nearly twenty Forgotten. But each time we killed one, a hundred more replaced it.

"They never stop coming." I said breathlessly.

"They're pushing us back to the gates. I need to find my father so we may start evacuating the woman and children out of the kingdom."

"Go. I'll start looking for my comrades."

She nodded her head to me and I began to feel the magic within the air ripple around us. The woman that stood before me began to morph into a wolf. The creature dropped to all fours before me, we were eye-level with one another. She blinked her round almond eyes at me before turning around and racing through the battle field. The white wolf soon disappeared from view.

I went in search for Estel and Haimera, crying out their names desperately. I feared that I might stumble upon their corpses but I pushed that fear away, they were strong warriors and they would survive. Finally, someone answered my calls.

"Arendella!" I heard a voice cry out but I couldn't tell if it was male or female. I ran in the direction of the voice and found who I had been searching for.

"Estel! Haimera!" I cried out joyously as I rushed toward them.

Both of them were coated in tar and they were both pushed to their limits. Their bodies grew tired. I peered around us searching for the one person that was missing from their small group. "Where is Renier?"

Estel and Haimera gazed at one another. Haimera answered, "We have not seen him since the battle started."

"He is probably fighting alongside Uthtor then." I said.

"We must find Uthtor and Lone Claw. The king's army is pushing us back toward the gates." Estel said.

"Crescent has went in search for Lone Claw so that they may start evacuating the women and children."

"She shall not find him in time to do so. Let us begin the evacuation." Haimera said.

"Then we shall do so." I said.

We each nodded to one another and began to make our way toward the gates. Forgotten stood in our way, trying desperately to slaughter anyone who was not a part of the king's army. They outnumbered us, there were simply too many of them. But we fought.

Just like the battle at Menanor; Estel, Haimera, and I fell into sync with one another. Our attacks, our minds becoming one. Though our formation and fighting skills were great our bodies and minds were tired. And the Forgotten never stopped attacking. One after another they continued their relentless attacks. We found ourselves completely surrounded. We attempted to fight back to back but a Forgotten had jumped in between us and separated me from Estel and Haimera. I found myself trying to fight off so many of the Forgotten but there were too many. My arms burned with the constant strain of attacks.

Then, before I realized it, a Forgotten had swept my feet from underneath me using its staff. I fell to the hard ground. I gazed up at the creature as it raised its staff above its head. I knew the hit would be fatal but there was nothing I could do. So, I accepted my death. As the staff began to fall toward me a golden mass blurred my vision and the shrieks of the creature filled my ears. Haimera stood in front of me, her golden dress, singed and frayed, road along the currents of the wind. The dagger end of her golden staff was coated in tar. Then she turned her cat-like gaze upon me. "It's about time I pay off my debuts to you for saving my life." She said with a smile.

Once we had fought off our horde of Forgotten we found Lone Claw fighting alongside Uthtor. Lone Claw was an older looking man, seeming to be of the same age as Uthtor. His long gray hair was braided down his back. One of his gray wolf ears was cut, the very tip of the ear was missing. Then his black as coal eyes landed upon us as we approached. Crescent had also approached them, still in her wolf form. Once she was close to the men she shifted back to her, almost, human form.

"Father, we must evacuate the women and children. The archers cannot hold the Forgotten off much longer, there are too many climbing over the gates." Her white ears flickered as her tail swayed behind her.

"As soon as the gates are opened they will swarm into the kingdom. We simply cannot risk the seal in order to save the people."

"There must be another way. We cannot sacrifice their lives, for it is not our right to do so." Crescent said.

Lone Claw thought for a minute, his brows creasing together. His gray tail swishing uneasily behind him. "The Forgotten are only after the seal. Move all the people toward the back of the kingdom and have them climb the gates. We'll have them hide in the forest until the battle is over." He then gazed upon us, "Crescent I need you to take this group of people with you and guard the seal. Climb over the gates on the east side."

"As you wish father." She bowed.

Just before we set off toward Cyfaserin the king rode into battle. His black stallion seeming as though it were charging toward us. The king slashed his sword through the air as he bellowed loudly. Lone Claw and Uthtor stood before us, their broad backs facing us.

"Go. We shall hold him off." Lone Claw spoke in a low voice.

Without protesting we ran toward the gates. Crescent running alongside us in her wolf form. The gates were in sight and we made our way toward the east side of the kingdom. Crescent approached the gates, the air around her shifting as she morphed into her human form.

"I'll be the first to climb the gates. Since this is your first time in Cyfaserin you will have to follow me. Do not stray from the paths that I guide you along."

With that her hands gripped the wooden gates and she began her climb. One by one we climbed after her, me being the last to make sure that no Forgotten had followed us. Once I was standing at the top of the gates I leaped down and landed with a soft thud, dust wafting into the air as my feet landed upon the dirt ground.

"Now, let us begin evacuating the women and children. Any man you find send them into battle. They are very capable of fighting so do not let them fool you into thinking they are too weak to fight."

She turned her back to us and led us toward a small town within the kingdom. It was quiet. No one was outside in the streets, it seemed as though this place had been deserted years ago. Crescent walked toward the first small cottage, gently she knocked upon the door. A few moments later a young girl peaked her head outside. Her large brown eyes staring upon us. Crescent knelt down to the ground making herself eye-level with the young girl.

"Where is your mother, young pup?"

The girl spoke not a word, only pointing her finger inside the house.

"May I come in and speak with her?"

The girl hesitated for a moment but then an older woman approached the door. Her short cut, black hair framed around her face. Her black ears and tail twitched uneasily. She looked upon Crescent with sorrowful eyes.

"Have you come to tell me that my husband is dead?" Her voice cracked.

"No, that is not why I'm here. I've come to start evacuating the women and children. My father has asked that everyone climb the gates at the back of the kingdom and to hide in the forest until the battle is over."

The woman gazed down at her daughter. The little girl clung onto her mother's dress as she stood behind her. "Alright." Was all the women said.

When we approached the next house a young man answered the door.

"Why are you not in battle? You're 21, are you not?"

"I'm sorry but I had to stay behind to watch over my younger sister and brother. Our father went into battle and I couldn't leave them alone."

Just then two little children approached the door. They looked almost exactly alike, they had to be twins due to their looks and they seemed to be of the same age.

"Where is your mother?"

The boy looked down upon the ground, "She passed away five years ago."

Crescent's fist clenched by her sides, "I am sorry. I am here to evacuate everyone out of the kingdom, be sure to follow me. Keep your brother and sister close to you and watch over them."

"Thank you, Princess Crescent." The young man bowed and gathered his family.

As we walked along the dirt streets toward more cottages I noticed that Crescent seemed to be lost in her own world, deep in her thoughts. I approached her and gently placed my hand upon her shoulder. "Crescent, are you alright?"

She snapped out of her thoughts and returned to our world. "Yes, I am alright." With that she marched toward another house gathering another family.

*   *   *   *

"That should be everyone." Crescent said as we stood before the gates at the back of the kingdom. She turned around and gazed upon the people that were gathered before her. "Now, you all must climb the gates and wait in the forest until the battle is over. No matter what you hear or see never come out of hiding unless Lone Claw or I or any of the people that stand with me tell you to do so. Understood?"

Everyone nodded their heads and one by one they climbed the gates. Mothers helped their young ones by giving them a boost up and if the kids were too small they clung onto their mothers back as they ascended the wooden gates. Once everyone made it safely over the gates Crescent led us toward the castle.

"Within this castle lies the fourth seal."

Just as those words slipped out of her mouth the entrance gates burst open and a flood of Forgotten entered into the kingdom. The archers tried their best to take out as many as they could but no matter how many they killed the Forgotten never stopped coming. Finally, the archers tossed their bows down and shifted. Hundreds of wolves dropped to the ground and locked the Forgotten in battle, giving us more time to find the seal.

Once we entered the castle we followed Crescent as she walked toward the throne that sat at the far end of the room. Behind the throne hung a massive red tapestry with a grey wolf stitched into the fabric.

"I don't see the seal. Where is it?" Haimera asked curiously.

Crescent turned and faced Haimera with a smirk upon her face, then turning around she moved aside the tapestry that hung behind the throne. And there behind the fabric was a wooden door. "Behind this door is where the seal is hidden."

Just as Crescent was reaching out to open the door Estel stopped her. "Wait, every time we have gone into the room where the seal is hidden the king always finds it. Let us stay here and protect it."

"Good idea, Estel." Crescent said as she moved the tapestry over the door once more.

We then moved ourselves to the center of the room and waited for the king to make his entrance. My eyes stared upon the wooden doors as anxiety ate away at me. Fear clawed at my being. So many thoughts rushed through my mind.

What if I was taken prisoner again?
What if he kills one of the people I care most about?
What will happen if this seal is destroyed?

"Crescent, there is something I've always wondered about you Cyfasin people. Is it alright to ask you a question?" Haimera asked out of genuine curiosity.

"You may."

"How did you and your people acquire the magic that aids you in your transformation to your wolf form?"

Crescent smiled at this question, seeming as though Haimera would be the first to ask her this. "Our true form is not our human form, the wolf inside us is. Long ago, the first clan leader, Shadow Bringer, was nothing but a mere wolf. No human form he could transform into. It is said that while he was out hunting in the woods he stumbled upon a human whose magic was said to be very powerful. The human was mortally wounded due to a bear attack and just as the bear was about to make its last, fatal blow Shadow Bringer attacked the bear, saving the human. It is said that the human was so grateful that he bestowed upon Shadow Bringer the magic of transformation and that magic he passed on to the rest of his clan. And that magic has run through our blood lines ever since."

Haimera stared upon Crescent with admiration and wonder. The wolf princess then smiled at the curious halfling, causing Haimera's cheeks to fluster a faint red.

We each had gotten so lost in Crescent's tale that we had not noticed that the king himself waited for us at the wooden doors. Claps echoed throughout the throne room as he approached us with a smile upon his lips.

"Ah, I do enjoy a great story. Please, tell me another one princess of the wolves." He bowed extending one arm out to the side.

"Here's another one for you; There was once an evil king whose last day on this earth was today." Crescent said as the air around her began to ripple. Her body morphed into that of a great white wolf.

"I have to say that I do not like the ending of that story. Perhaps I can change it." As he said this he drew his sword from its sheath. The sword's hisses filled the air.

The king's crimson eyes wondered around the room until they landed upon me. His lips curled back into a malicious smile, baring his sharpened teeth as his reptilian tongue ran across them. "Ah, Arendella it's been quite some time has it not? I do say that I miss that sweet scent of yours, it's so... enticing."

I glanced over to my right at Estel. His face was creased with anger an anger I have never seen before on him. And it frightened me. Estel moved to stand in front of me.

"Stay behind me Arendella."

"No, I can fight as well." I said as I took my place beside him.

Haimera then moved to stand beside me and Crescent took her place beside Haimera.

Hope blossomed in my heart. It wasn't just the three of us, now we had Crescent. Four against one. We had the upper hand this time.

FIGHT
CHAPTER 12

"You fools still think you stand a chance against me? Have you still not learned that you shall *never* be strong enough to defeat me!" Andakile strode toward us. "With a flick of my wrist I could send you flying across the room, like this." He flicked his hand in the air and Crescent was sent flying to the other side of the room. Her body slammed into the stone wall, a quiet whimper escaped her. Shakenly she stood from the ground. Her right hind leg had been injured and blood trickled from the wound. But then a faint glow of golden light wrapped around her leg and soon enough her wound had been healed.

"Ah, I forgot that you Cyfasin people are excellent healers." Andakile seemed to admire this but annoyance also clouded his gaze.

Crescent snarled and then charged at the king. He raised his sword into the air ready to strike it down upon the wolf's head.

"Camela o' fenier!" Haimera cried out.

Blazing hot fire was summoned from the crystal atop her staff. It sizzled and crackled within the air as it raced toward the king. Quickly he swept up his cloak to block the flames. Once the flames had died out I made eye contact with the king, a smirk wrote itself upon his lips. He had crafted himself a new cloak in the time since our last battle. Then our gazes broke from one another as Crescent wrapped her powerful jaws around Andakile's arm. His shouts echoed around the room. Her teeth sunk into his skin causing black tar to ooze from the wound she caused.

"Damn you! You, filthy dog!" A blast of magic sent her flying across the room once more.

"Deitie no' teinie!" I chanted quickly.

A translucent orb enveloped the wolf before her body slammed into the wall. Slowly the wolf was brought back down to the ground safely and unharmed. Crescent bowed her head to me, thanking me.

"Each of you are becoming a nuisance." Andakile extended his hand in our direction. The grey skin of his palm exposed. There was a shift in the air as he summoned his magic. A cloud of red mist began to radiate from his being and a black mass began to form within the air between his out stretched hand. Clouds of tentacles began to crawl along the ground toward Haimera and I.

"What sort of magic is this?" Haimera questioned in disbelief.

"Forbidden. It's the magic that he's stolen from the seals." I answered her.

"Well aren't you the smart one, Arendella." The king's crimson eyes glowed.

Haimera and I quickly called upon our magic, summoning forth a force field. The mists of tentacles inched their way toward us and crawled onto our force fields. They pounded against our magic trying to break it. As their attacks became more forceful cracks began to manifest in our force fields. Soon they would shatter.

"Your shields won't hold up much longer. You'll have to face me eventually." He taunted us.

Then, with one final blow our fields shattered and the tentacles wrapped themselves around us, holding us within the air. The dark magic that radiated from them seemed to have an effect on Haimera and I. It felt as though it was draining our energy, our magic.

Suddenly a bright green blast of magic slammed into the king, causing him to stumble backwards. His magic on us wavered and we were able to break free. Haimera and I landed upon the ground with a soft thud, thankfully it wasn't too far of a fall. Quickly I snatched our staffs from the ground and tossed Haimera hers.

"Thank you for the save, Estel." Haimera said to him with gratefulness.

"Indeed, thank you Estel."

"Anything for my love." He smiled sweetly to me.

"Enough of this nonsense!" Andakile shouted as he charged toward us. The red mist around his body grew more intense, it began to morph and form into tentacles. As he approached the tentacles began to grab at us. Three of them raced toward me, snatching at the empty air where I once stood. Suddenly the room was lit up with lighting. The bolts danced around striking anything that got in their way. My gaze landed upon Haimera as she continued her merciless attack of lighting.

"Haimera stop! The room is too small for us to call upon lighting, we shall be struck as well!"

Immediately she ceased her attacks, calling back the lighting. I began to sort through my memories of every magical attack I had memorized. Then one stood out to me. Raising my staff into the air I slammed the end of it down upon the ground before me.

"Ethiara oath' no'thelera!" I chanted loudly.

Suddenly the earth beneath my feet began to rumble, the marble flooring began to crack. Then vines blasted through the floor. They reached high up to the ceiling. They danced behind me waiting for me to give them a command of attack. Andakile smirked as he stared upon me. He stood at the center of the room, the tentacles behind his back began to grow until they touched the ceiling.

Perfect. A fight between him and I so that he'll be too distracted to fend off the rest of our group. But suddenly the room rippled and a red dome of mist clouded around us. Estel rushed forward but was stopped by the dome.

"I wouldn't want anyone to disturb us. So now it's a fight between you and I." A malicious smirk wrote itself upon his scared red lips. He flashed his sharpened teeth at me. "Come, show me that power you possess!"

His tentacles raced through the air toward me, fortunately my vines blocked his attack before they came an inch closer. Behind me I could hear Haimera, Estel, and Crescent attacking the dome. Trying to come to my aid. Lighting thundered loudly as it struck the dome but nothing happened. Not even a scratch.

"Their efforts are meaningless, nothing can destroy my dome." He cackled.

While he was too busy speaking nonsense I sent my vines forth, they whipped at him but his tentacles blocked the attack. Together they danced within the air wrapping around one another. The tentacles began to tug and pull at the vines, uprooting them from the ground. This constant strain of magic was draining my energy. I didn't know how much longer I could keep this up.

Suddenly the floor between Andakile and I began to rumble and crack. An explosion caused the marble flooring to fly into the air and dust obscured my vision. I released my magic on the vines and quickly called forth a shield of protection. Debris crashed against my shield, cracking it. Once the dust had settled down I could finally see the cause of the explosion. Together Haimera, Estel, and Crescent stood before me. Haimera used her magic to dig a hole beneath the dome. Brilliant.

Together we stood and faced the king with our staffs ready and onward we charged toward him. Estel and Crescent led the main attacks, getting close enough to him to wound him. While Haimera and I stayed just far enough behind to unleash a strain of magical attacks. We sent forth fire and blasts of magic pulsating toward him. Our magic slammed into his body with such force that it blew him backward causing him to slam into the dome that he created. Estel and Crescent rushed toward him and attacked while he was still weak from our attack. Estel stabbed at the king numerous times with the dagger end of his staff. Crescent's teeth sunk themselves into his calf attempting to rip his leg from his body.

"I have had enough of your foolishness!" Andakile shouted as his body began to radiate a red glow and a blast of magic sent Estel and Crescent flying into the air.

Their bodies landed upon the ground with heavy thuds. I quickly rushed over to Estel's side. "My love, are you alright?" I asked trembling with fear.

"As long as your with me I shall be alright." But his face creased with pain. I noticed his hand was clenching at his side. Gently I moved his hand aside to expose a bloody wound.

"Estel, you are wounded."

"Arendella, we'll distract Andakile long enough for you to heal him." Haimera said to me.

"Thank you."

Once they took off down the room after Andakile I quickly set to work healing Estel.

"Thela pam'ala namos!" Faint glittering wisps of air emerged from the crystal upon my staff. They danced around, riding along the air until they disappeared into his wound. The area where he was injured began to glow and his skin began to lace itself back together once more.

Once he was back on his feet we rushed to help Haimera and Crescent. Andakile's tentacles had a hold on Haimera, repeatedly slamming her body into the ground. Blood began to weep from her head. It seemed as though consciousness had slipped away from her. A few more times of being slammed into the ground and she would be gone, forever. I was not going to allow that to happen. Quickly calling upon my powers I sent forth a blast of magic. Bright purple light radiated from it as it demolished the tentacle that was holding Haimera. As she was falling to the ground Estel quickly acted and caught her.

"Lay her down and I'll put up a shield to protect her." I told him. Once she was on the ground a force field shielded her body from further harm.

Now, only three of us remained to fight against Andakile. I knew Crescent couldn't keep fighting like this, she was too injured but she fought just like the strong warrior she was. Estel and I could barely manage to call forth much more magic and fighting the king without it would be nearly impossible.

A loud whimper snapped my attention over to Crescent. King Andakile had her body wrapped up in his tentacles. They began to glow brighter and I began to notice that Crescent's body slowly was being transformed into her human self. Soon that blonde haired warrior stared into the king's face with anger.

"Damn you to hell and may you burn for eternity!" She shouted.

Estel and I ran to her aid but the king stopped us. His magic smashed us against the wall, knocking our staffs from our grasp. But we found that we could not move, his magic held us to the wall.

"Now, Princess of the Wolves, tell me where the seal is."

"You think I would reveal the seal's location to you? You are mistaken."

"What if I killed off your friends one by one? Would that change your mind?"

Crescent's face no longer showed anger but fear. And that fear would cause her to give up the location of the seal.

"Don't tell him! Our lives aren't worth the lives of thousands!" I cried out to her.

"Maybe I should start with Arendella." Andakile said as his reptilian tongue ran across his sharpened teeth. He called my body forth. Bringing me face to face with him. His eyes glowed crimson. He smirked as his tongue ran across my cheek. My body trembled with repulsion. Then his tentacles wrapped around my arms and legs, hoisting me into the air.

"This shall be a very slow and painful death. Though it saddens me that I couldn't get a taste of your pureness Arendella."

The tentacles tightened themselves around my arms and legs, the pressure felt as though it would break my bones but slowly the tentacles began to pull. Slowly tugging my bones from their sockets. I could feel my shoulder dislocating. A scream welled up inside my throat and echoed around the room. Sweat beaded down my brow. Pain enveloped my being. Rippling down into my soul. Still, the tentacles tugged at my body trying to tear me apart piece by piece. Then my other shoulder popped out of place. Tears burned my cheeks as screams of agony escaped from my throat. Estel yelled my name and cursed the king as he tried to break free from the magic that was holding him.

"Stop this! Please!" Crescent cried out in panic. "I'll tell you where the seal is!"

I barely had the strength to lift my head to face her. "P-Please Crescent, don't reveal its location. My life holds no meaning compared to the seal."

"Your life holds more meaning than you may think, Arendella." With that Crescent faced the king. "I shall tell you."

He smiled wickedly, "Good girl."

Crescent turned her head toward the throne, "There behind the tapestry is a door and there you shall find the seal."

"Crescent..." I said sorrowfully as my gaze wondered down to the ground. We had failed, again. Dread consumed me. Only one seal remained, Theleshara's.

What chance did we have at stopping the king from destroying the final seal?

Then Crescent and I were flung upon the ground as if we were nothing. My body was crippled with pain. I cried out in agony as my body met with the marble floor.

The dome around us fell as Andakile approached the throne. His tentacles reached out and tore the tapestry down. He then entered into the room that contained the fourth seal. The sounds of it shattering rang in my ears as a faint red light emanated from the doorway behind the throne.

"I am so sorry." Crescent said in sorrow, tears weeping from her brown eyes.

"I-I would have done the same if I was in your place." The words I spoke were true.

But now four seals had been destroyed. Three of which were my fault because I was too weak to stop him. Now, he would destroy Theleshara and its seal.

RETURN OF SHAME
CHAPTER 13

As we approached the silver gates of Theleshara all sorts of emotions swarmed me at once; dread, despair, failure. All those words circled around in my mind like a tornado. A negative whirlwind that consumed my mind.

Once we entered into the kingdom we were greeted by many elves that lined along the streets, hoping to hear news of victory. Sadly, they would not be receiving that news. They gathered from the looks upon our faces that we had lost the battle. That we had lost many people and that we had lost another seal. Their hopeful gazes turned to that of dread. My stomach turned as I looked upon the faces of the disappointed elves.

When the horses were led to their stables and Uthtor escorted his remaining soldiers to the barracks Estel, Haimera, and I were left with the duty of informing the queen of our failure. We ascended the marble steps and pushed open the crystal doors. Soon we found ourselves before the queen. She stood from her throne as we approached and waited for our news. This time I was not to be the one to inform her. Instead, Estel stepped forward.

"My queen, I am sorry to inform you of this but we lost another seal."

The room was enveloped in silence, it blanketed itself around our beings. Queen Lyanthian spoke not a word but disappointment was etched across her face. Her hazel gaze watched us closely until her eyes landed upon me. I felt as though she blamed me for this failure but I couldn't be upset with that. For I believe that it was entirely my fault. There were so many things I could have done if I were only stronger. Tears prickled in my eyes and I had to turn my gaze down to the floor.

"And now the king shall come here. But I can tell from the necklace hanging from your neck, Arendella, that your journey went well." With that, she left the room, leaving a trail of despair behind her.

I slipped away from the throne room wishing to be alone but when I entered into the hallway that led to my room I found Renier standing beside my door. I wanted to turn my back on him and walk away but I couldn't bring myself to do so. Instead, I approached him. His gaze met with mine. Those honey colored eyes of his had purple bruises blossoming beneath them. It seemed as though he hadn't slept for days.

"Why are you here?" My question sounded harsher than I meant for it to.

"The last we spoke we left off not on good terms. I wanted to apologize for my behavior." He took a step closer to me.

Instinct told me to take a few steps back from him.

"You look upon me with fear. Why?" Once more he advanced toward me. His hands reached out for me. His eyes seemed to crave for... something.

"I think you should retire to your room for the night, you might have come down with something or possibly drank too much wine." I said as I tried to enter my room.

He yanked my arm from my door and forced me against the wall. My body was still sore from what Andakile had done to me, magic healed my bones but my body was still recovering. My arm ached in protest as his grasp tightened around it. There was a crazed look within his gaze. Like something had driven him mad.

"Renier, release me now."

"Arendella, allow me another chance to win your love. That elf isn't suited for you." He leaned in close to me, he breathed in my scent. His lips almost tracing along the skin of my neck. "You know I can sense a darkness burning inside of you, though the flame may be small it is still there."

My skin began to crawl. The urge to run took over my body. Quickly I yanked my arm from his grasp, shoved him aside, and locked myself in my room. I summoned upon my magic to insure that he wouldn't be able to come inside my chamber. Though it did not block out the sounds of his shouts and knocking. This was not the Renier I grew up with. Now, he was a complete stranger.

*   *   *   *

I had been locked in my room since our return. My mind was plagued with darkness. It seeped into my brain. The king's magic was working its hold on me once more. Its evil coursing through my veins. I could feel the skin on my arm burning as though someone were carving into it with hot iron.

Carefully, I rolled up my sleeve to see a bloody symbol carved into my skin. The fresh blood oozed from the wound. The king had marked me as his. My head hung low with burden. But doing this would keep Arendella safe from harm. I cared not of anyone else's safety, their lives meant nothing to me.

I pressed my hands hard against my temples. These thoughts were not my own. It was the king's cruel magic forcing me to think in such a way. A scream of frustration rose in my throat but I silenced it. Wanting no one to hear my cries.

No longer were my thoughts my own.

No longer were my actions my own.

The sound of footsteps echoed throughout the hallway and I knew it was Arendella returning to her room. Suddenly it felt like something had taken ahold of my mind. Controlling me. I tried to fight against it but to no avail. My feet were moving on their own and I found myself in the hallway standing before Arendella's door. Soon her white-lilac hair came into view. When she approached me I found that the words coming from my mouth were not my own. I tried to fight the force that had taken control over my body, I tried to retreat back into my room but nothing worked no matter how hard I fought. Soon she was looking upon me in a way that made my heart sink. Her gaze was written in fear. The girl I loved feared me.

* * * *

I must have fallen asleep sometime during the night because a knocking upon my door had awaken me. The sun's early morning rays shone brightly in my room almost blinding me, my eyes still needed time to adjust to the light. Once more the person knocked upon my door. Quickly I jumped out of my bed and instantly regretted that decision. The quick movements caused my head to grow dizzy, my body swayed as I approached the door.

"Who's there?" I called out.

"Estel." His voice sounded from the other side of the door.

Once the door was unlocked I opened it to see his handsome face staring down upon me. He stepped into my room, closed the door behind him, and cupped his hands around my face. His thumbs gently traced along the skin upon my cheeks. Those ocean blue eyes of his radiated with love. Those lips of his pulled themselves into a heart-warming smile that melted my heart. Though our journeys were separate and we weren't apart for long I had still missed him.

"Your door is normally never locked. Why was it today?"

"Renier gave me a freight last night. He probably had a little too much wine or something."

Anger lit a flame in his ocean gaze, "Do you wish for me to speak with him?"

"No, that won't be necessary."

Once we had stopped speaking of Renier, the tenderness in Estel's gaze returned. His hands moved from my face and slid down to my hips. When his hands gripped me tightly I couldn't help but wince at the pain. My body was still recovering.

"My Love, you are still hurt. I must apologize, I should have known that your body still ached from what that king did to you."

My mind then began to swarm with memories from what had happened. The image of my body being held in the air by those tentacles was burned into my mind. I could still feel them around my arms and legs, pulling and pulling until my bones popped out of place. My body trembled at the memory. It haunted me.

Estel gripped my trembling hands in his and gently placed a tender kiss upon them. The softness of his lips traced along my skin. Though his kisses stopped the trembling they didn't stop the memories.

* * * *

I sat upon a chair next to a window staring out into the quiet night. My gaze locked in the direction of Raz'noak, expecting to see the king's army marching its way here. I brought the glass up to my lips savoring the taste of the wine that entered into my mouth. Soon I felt another presence enter into my room, without peering to see who it was I said, "Good evening, Uthtor."

"Good evening, Lyanthian." He bowed.

"Are your soldiers prepared for the coming battle?"

"They are as strong as ever."

I sighed, "I meant not in strength. I meant are they prepared mentally? Prepared to lose their lives? Lose their loved ones?" I stared solemnly into the red liquid as it swished around in my glass.

"You seem to be prepared." He said concerned.

I turned to face him with a smile of sorrow, "You must always be prepared for the worst."

"No matter how much you may think you're prepared, when the moment comes you are never truly prepared for it."

"Ah, Uthtor. Just as wise as ever." I said shaking my head as a small chuckle escaped me.

Uthtor approached me and placed a hand upon my shoulder. "You were never prepared for what happened so many years ago."

My gaze returned to window. "No one can be prepared to lose their lover and it isn't something you ever come to peace with."

"You still think of him don't you?"

"Everyday." My heart beat with sorrow and I could feel tears rising in my eyes.

"The king shall pay for every bad deed he has ever done."

"His payment cannot come soon enough. A war is approaching and we must all prepare ourselves." I said as I rose from my chair and stepped out onto the balcony.

"For the worst?" He questioned.

Our gazes met, "For the worst."

*   *   *   *

"The queen has been distant with us since our return." Haimera said.

We decided to take an early morning stroll through the castle gardens, everything was still covered in snow. The frozen ground crunched under our feet as we walked along the path, creating trails of foot prints behind us.

"I blame her distance on our failure." The words left my lips more harshly than I meant for them to.

My words did not seem to faze her, she seemed to agree with them. "The king is too powerful now. I fear that we shall lose the coming battle." Her emerald eyes stared solemnly into the grey winter's sky.

"I fear that as well."

My friendship with Haimera has grown so much since our first meeting. For so long I had feared allowing people to get close to me but now I'm grateful for this friendship I had with her. Now I had a friend to confide in. Though, we haven't spoken about our kiss. But I think she preferred to not speak of it so I didn't bring it up in conversation.

Soon we came upon the end of the garden path and a good distance away from us we saw Uthtor's soldiers preparing for battle. Training until their bodies were drenched in sweat and still they pushed themselves. Then they broke off into small groups and began to run laps around the castle grounds. As I watched them I couldn't help but think I should be training as hard as them. Making myself stronger.

"Haimera, why don't we train like them?" I said nodding my head in their direction.

She made a considering look as she watched the soldiers. Then she gave an approving nod of her head. "Alright. How about we meet up before dawn tomorrow?"

My gaze returned to the soldiers. "Before dawn."

TRAINING
CHAPTER 14

As promised I met Haimera in the castle garden before dawn. Though I arrived a little late, the sun was beginning to peak over the horizon. The sun's rays bathed Haimera in a heavenly glow. She had pulled her long, ebony hair back into the style of braid that snaked down her back. She wore a long-sleeved black shirt, tight fitted black pants, and boots. Within her hands she grasped two long, wooden sticks that were the same height as her.

When I approached her she smiled and tossed one of the sticks to me. "Sparring?"

"Indeed."

She then took her stance, bending one knee in front of her other leg and grasping the stick with both hands. She raised one ebony eyebrow to me as a smirk wrote itself upon her plump lips.

Her stick swept toward my feet but I was quick and leaped into the air, dodging her attack. Then I brought my stick down toward her but she was quick to counter my attack. Her stick smacked against mine and soon we stood face to face using all our strength to knock the other off their feet. My arms burned with the continuous use of my muscles. So I forced my staff harder against hers, her feet began to slide across the ground leaving trail of upturned earth. Then she planted her feet into the ground and maneuvered herself to where she now stood beside me. Our gazes locked as she struck at my side, the wood cracked against my ribcage sending a rippling pain through my body.

Instead of letting the attack slow me, I regained my position and struck at her legs, sweeping them from beneath her. She went tumbling down to the ground. But she refused to fall alone. Her stick slammed into the backs of my knees and I fell with her, landing beside her. We lay there breathless staring into the grey morning sky.

"I'm going to miss this." Haimera said breathlessly.

"Miss what? Beating the life out of one another?"

Haimera chuckled. "Maybe. But I mean I will miss the fighting, the training. All this gave me a purpose. What am I when the war is over? I shall no longer be a warrior."

"You have the heart and soul of a warrior, that shall never change. You shall have purpose when this is all over."

She stood from the ground, brushed her pants off, and stretched her slender arms toward the sky. "Let's start doing laps around the castle."

She took off at a brisk jog with me trailing just behind her. Her ebony braid whipped through the air. She left behind a trail of foot prints through the snow.

I kept my distance behind her. My breathing was heavy. Clouds of air escaped my mouth as the hot breath touched the cold air. I could feel my calves burning and aching but I still pushed myself to run. We rounded around toward the entrance of the castle and took a sharp turn, continuing our jog.

As I was running alongside her, I stared into her face. She looked so determined, so concentrated. She was pushing herself way beyond her limits. Her face was tinted a bright red, cheeks a faint rosy color. Thin tendrils of ebony hair wisped free from her braid. Her lips chapped. Once we rounded around the other side of the castle Haimera stopped. She knelt over bracing her hands against her knees. She hung her head low as she struggled to catch her breath.

"Haimera, we can rest if you like." I said as I leaned against the marble wall of the castle.

"N-No. I'm fine. We still have more training to do."

I stood beside her and placed a hand upon her shoulder. "A few moments of rest and we can continue our training."

"Alright." She stretched her body and leaned against the castle. "You know it's different when you're fighting on the battlefield. You're so focused on living and fighting that you aren't focused on the pain or how tired your body is." Her eyes stared into the sky.

"Why do you push yourself so hard?"

She looked upon me with a smile, "I could ask you the same question, Arendella." When I didn't respond to her she cocked her head to the side, "You think I haven't noticed?"

A sigh escaped my lips and I watched as my hot breath rose into the sky. "I want to be able to protect everyone I love. I failed two people and refuse to fail anyone else that I hold dear." My hand reached up and grasped the crystal that hung from my necklace. My thumb glided across its smooth, cool surface.

Haimera nodded her head and stepped away from the castle wall.

"Now, let's continue our training, shall we? Or as you like to call it, beating the life out of one another."

*   *   *   *

My legs burned with each step I took up the stairs. My calves ached in protest as I ascended up the spiraling staircase. Finally, I had reached the hallway that led to my room. Once my door was pushed open Estel's face came into view. He was sat at the end of my bed, waiting for me to return.

"How was your training with Haimera?"

I groaned as I sat beside him. "My body aches. I don't think I've ever trained so hard in my life."

He chuckled and began to massage my shoulders, applying slight but gentle pressure. His hands then moved down to my back and his knuckles kneaded into my aching bones.

"Your body is still recovering love, you shouldn't have pushed yourself so hard." He said concerned.

"I know. But right now I'm glad to be here with you." I turned to face him and placed a tender kiss upon his lips.

"Would you like for me to run a hot bath for you? It might relieve your aching muscles."

"That would be amazing, thank you Estel."

"Anything for my love." He placed a kiss upon my brow and entered into my bathing room and began drawing water for a bath. "It's ready." He called from the room.

Once I began to undress he turned to leave. "Estel." He stopped at the door when I called out to him. I approached him, wrapping my arms around his waist as I kissed his back. "Don't leave." I whispered to him.

He turned to face me, his fingertips lightly traced over the bare skin of my arms as he bent down to kiss me. As our lips locked I tugged at his shirt wanting to feel his body against mine once more. He pulled his shirt over his head and tossed it upon the marble floor. His muscular arms wrapped around me as he lifted me and pressed me against the wall. My legs snaked around his body as my fingers tangled themselves in his blonde hair. His soft lips placed delicate kisses along my neck. A flash of heat rushed through my body with each kiss. A moan rose in my throat. My body thrummed with pleasure. Estel's lips met with mine once more, locking them in a passionate kiss. He then carried me over to the bath, releasing his hold on me so that he may remove his trousers.

I turned my back to him as I entered into the steaming water, dipping one foot in followed by the rest of my body. I reached my hand to him, beckoning him to join me. He smiled and entered the bath. I snaked my arms around his neck as I pulled myself into his lap. My fingers ran through his hair as I stared into those ocean eyes of his, getting lost in his beautiful gaze. A smile formed upon his perfect lips. His fingertips trailed down my spine.

"Arendella, I love you with my body, heart, and soul." He whispered lovingly to me.

"I love you as well, Estel." Hearing those words escape my lips caused his smile to brighten.

"Forever." His lips whispered.

"Forever."

*   *   *   *

Early the next morning before daybreak, Haimera knocked upon my door calling me from my dreams. Another morning of training. I groaned at the thought, my muscles did as well. I turned over in my bed to be greeted by Estel's sleeping face. My fingers traced along his cheeks, brushing his golden hair away from his sleeping eyes. "I'll return soon my love." I whispered as I placed a kiss upon his cheek.

Slowly I climbed out of bed and began to dress for my morning training. I slid the black pants over my long legs and pulled the long sleeve shirt over my head. I laced up my boots and braided my hair. The white braid was striped with lilac. I traced my fingers over the lilac strands of hair. I began to wonder of my father and what Lyanthian was hiding from me. Haimera's knocking broke me from my thoughts and I finally left my room to join her for our training.

"Usually you meet me in the garden. Tell me why I had to wake you this morning? Did a certain someone keep you up all night?" She winked an emerald eye at me.

"Perhaps." I smiled to her as I led the way down the stairs.

She trailed behind me, our footsteps echoed around us as we descended down the staircase. "Arendella, does the coming battle not worry you?"

I stopped dead in my tracks and stared down the dark stairway. "It does. Why do you ask?" I questioned without facing her.

"It just seems as though you carry on through your day as if nothing worries you. How do you do it?"

"I have many worries, Haimera. But I do not let them show." And with that our conversation came to end and our walk continued in silence.

Finally, we walked into the castle garden to begin our training. Haimera stood before me, but not facing me. Her gaze was locked upon the rising sun. I stood beside her and watched as the sky lit up with hues of orange and yellow. The cool winter's breeze nipped at our skin as it blew past us.

"I do wonder how Crescent is doing. They lost many people in the battle and we didn't stay to help in anyway." Haimera said.

"Her father, Lone Claw, sent a letter to Lyanthian. Though they lost many people their will is not broken. They have buried their dead and mourned them respectfully."

"We should pay them a visit, soon would be lovely but we have a battle approaching and we must be here for when it arrives. Though, I must admit it would be nice to see Crescent again." The corners of her pink lips pulled into a smile.

"It would be nice to see her." I said as I watched Haimera.

*   *   *   *

The following day while Haimera and I were doing our morning training a group of people approached the castle. From where we stood it was hard to tell who these people were. We couldn't see their faces. Queen Lyanthian soon stepped out of the castle and greeted the gathered group of people. After a greeted exchange she led them inside the castle. Haimera and I peered at each other curiously and walked toward the castle.

Once we entered into the throne room the people peered over their shoulders upon our arrival. It was Crescent and her father, Lone Claw. They were accompanied by three other people. The golden haired warrior smiled to us and approached us, her father nodded a greeting our way and continued his talk with Lyanthian.

"I'm glad to see you are back. I heard of your capture." Crescent said to me.

"How is everything in Cyfaserin?"

She peered down at the floor. "We've had to rebuild. When the Forgotten entered into our kingdom they destroyed many homes and stores. I'm glad we were able to get the women and children out of there in time."

"I'm sorry we were not there to aid you in the rebuilding of your kingdom." Haimera said apologetically.

Crescent placed a hand upon Haimera's shoulder. "Do not apologize. You had to attend to your dead and bring them home. We understand."

Haimera's cheeks flustered a light pink at Crescent's touch.

"What brings you here to Theleshara?" I asked.

The Cyfasin warrior broke her gaze away from Haimera's flustered face, "My father is requesting some supplies and food since everything was destroyed."

"Could he not send a letter requesting such?"

"He could have but I highly insisted on coming here. Once I heard of your safe return I wanted to see you." She glanced over at Haimera, "I wished to see you as well."

Queen Lyanthian and Lone Claw approached us. I bowed to the king of Cyfaserin, Haimera doing so as well. "There is no need for you to bow before me, Arendella. You are considered the princess of Theleshara."

I brought my gaze up to meet with his charcoal eyes, "But I don't hold the title nor do I claim it." Queen Lyanthian stared upon me as I spoke those words. We've had a disagreement in the past about this certain subject, but we hadn't spoken about it in years. "Plus, you are a king. I still wish to bow my respect to you."

His charcoal eyes gazed upon me as the grey wolf ears upon his head flickered. "If you wish to do so then I shall not stop you." He then turned to his daughter. "Crescent, the queen has offered us to stay for dinner. Would you like to do so?"

"We accept and thank you for your offer." She inclined her head to Lyanthian as her white tail swished happily behind her.

A little while later Haimera, Crescent, and I all gathered in my chamber. The Cyfasin warrior stretched her body out upon my bed, propping her head up upon her hand. I gazed upon the tribal tattoos that wrapped around her upper arm, the red color of them matched so well with her lightly tanned skin. Her tail swished through the air behind her and her auburn eyes shifted from Haimera to me.

"Why do you gaze upon us with curious eyes?" Haimera asked the wolf warrior.

"I am studying you two. You are both elves but your ears are slightly different than Arendella's. Why is that?" Crescent asked.

"That is because I am a halfling, born from an elf and a human."

"I haven't heard of such before but that may because I rarely leave Cyfaserin. They don't teach us much of other kingdoms and their history, we mostly learn the history of our people."

"Why do they not teach you of other kingdoms?" I didn't understand why they would refuse to teach them of the history of the land and many kingdoms.

"They believe there is no point in teaching us of other kingdoms histories if we do not live in them and are not of that race. They do not completely shelter us from all knowledge, we are aware of the different races such as; dwarves, fairy, human, and elves. But those are the only races we know of, we don't have knowledge of the mixed races." She sat up right crossing her legs over one another. "Since I am princess of the kingdom and the next in line for the throne I am taught some of the history of each kingdom. Though it is rare for me to leave my kingdom my father does take me to the other kingdoms to discuss supply trades and such."

Haimera was staring upon Crescent's tattoos curiously. Her eyes seeming to trace along them. Crescent caught Haimera's wondering eyes and chuckled. "Curious about my tattoos?" Her auburn eyes gazed down upon her arms, her tanned fingers glided across her inked skin. "Three lines wrapped around one's arm shows they are royalty." She glanced down at her own three lines. The first one was thick and as it got down to the last two they grew thinner. Of course there was a space between each one to separate them. "I was tattooed on my sixteenth birthday." She chuckled lightly, "One hell of a birthday present isn't it?"

"What do the two thick lines around your wrists mean?" Haimera pointed her dainty finger to Crescent's other tattoos.

"Two lines shows that you are a warrior. These are my most recent. I fought in my first battle a week ago. Once we had rebuilt everything one of the kingdoms elders tattooed me and many others."

"It's hard to believe that was your first battle. You fought like a highly skilled warrior." I said to her.

"We are trained at a very young age." There was a hint of something in her voice. "You don't get much of a childhood, especially being the daughter of the king. You spend most of your time practicing and learning the ways of the kingdom. How to be a proper queen. I didn't have many friends as a child." And that hint of something was sadness.

"I think some nice wine will lighten the mood and perhaps some sweets." Haimera smiled and left the room to fetch us a snack. I knew she was doing so in order to make Crescent feel better.

When I looked over at Crescent she was leaning toward me, she lightly sniffed the air around me. Her ears flickered. Her auburn eyes squinted as she stared upon me. She sat back and her eyes glided up and down my body while she crossed her arms over her chest.

"What is it?"

Her head cocked to the side. "You say you are elven, you even appear it, but I smell something different about you. You have a different smell than the other elves, a smell that makes you stand out from the rest." Her questioning gaze lingered upon me as she tried to figure out what was different about me, though I felt just like any other elf.

She did say it was rare for her to leave Cyfaserin. She must not be used to the scent of elves. With that thought in mind I brushed off what she had said.

Soon Haimera returned bringing with her a silver tray with three glasses, a bottle of wine, and three slices of cake. She set the tray down upon the bed in between Crescent and I. We sipped on our wine and ate our cakes quietly for some time until Haimera broke the silence.

"When Lone Claw considered you the princess of Theleshara Queen Lyanthian shot a strange glance at you, Arendella. Why was that?" She raised an ebony eyebrow as she fixed her cat-like gaze upon me.

I stared upon the red liquid within my glass as a sigh escaped my lips. "When I was seventeen the queen offered me the role of being the princess but I had rejected the idea. She didn't take too fondly of that."

"But why would you reject such an honorable title?"

"Because I felt as though it wasn't meant for me. The role of being a warrior felt more so like me. If I accepted the offer I knew that I would be made to stay out of battles. I had trained so hard for so many years I didn't want all of that to be put to waste." I sighed once more, "But despite my decline many of the people here think of me as their princess. Mostly because Queen Lyanthian adopted me as her daughter."

"I wish I could have declined such an offer. Being princess is a royal pain in the arse. Politics are one thing that I cannot stand. Plus, there are so many responsibilities given to you." Crescent sighed and rubbed the temples on her head.

"What responsibilities do you have?" Haimera asked.

"One of them being that I must give my blessing at every Cyfasin wedding. During trials I must place my vote on the fate of the person whom is being charged with an offense. I have to make sure that trades go smoothly between the kingdoms that we trade with in Lylanalian and overseas to the humans." She refilled her wine glass and took a sip before continuing the conversation. "It's hard to catch any alone time with all the servants following me around all day long, every day."

"I could only guess that it would be worse being the king or queen." I ran a finger around the ring on the top of my glass, still staring into the red liquid.

"I can tell you that it is worse. Between the politics, planning trades, keeping order within the kingdom, dealing with every problem that pops up, being the judge during every trial, and now recently battles, I'd rather stick with being the princess." She chugged down the remainder of her wine and placed the empty glass upon the tray.

"Let us move on to a more, lighter subject." Haimera gathered our glasses and plates on the tray and set it on the table. "Hmmm. I would like to get to know you better, Crescent." Then she fixed her emerald gaze upon me, "And I would wish to know more about you as well, Arendella."

Crescent propped her elbow up on her knee and placed her chin upon her hand, "What would you like to know?"

"What are you talents? Besides being a highly skilled warrior."

Crescent's golden eyebrows knitted together as she thought. "Well, being the princess I'm always busy rarely leaving me any leisure time. I'm talented with a sword that's about all the talent I have." She chuckled but then she seemed to realize something. "Oh! When I was younger I used to sing at festivals. I remember really enjoying it and sounding pretty decent."

"Do you not sing anymore?" Haimera asked.

"Unfortunately, my responsibilities as princess keep me very busy. They had to find someone else to take my spot during festivals." When she caught the sadness in Haimera and I's glances she quickly changed the subject away from her. "What about you, Haimera?"

"Oh, I can answer this for her." I gave a smirk to Haimera, "She has a talent for dancing. Especially when she's drunk."

Haimera playful slapped me on the arm, "I'm not *always* drunk when I dance but when it's a celebration and there's music plus alcohol I cannot help myself." She flipped her long ebony hair over her shoulder and placed her hand upon her chest, acting offended though I knew she was not. Crescent and I glanced at one another and giggles burst from us.

"Okay enough about my drunken talents, Arendella what is your talent? We've been friends for a while but you've never mentioned anything that you enjoyed doing."

"Well, I used to paint. My mother taught me as a child. Being the age I was people were genuinely surprised to see how talented I was in the art of painting. I loved it. Painting was a way for me to express myself. My mother and I would spend many hours painting together." A smile twitched at the corners of my lips.

"Then why do you not paint anymore?" Haimera questioned me.

A lump rose in my throat. "After my mother and sister were killed I never painted again. With the death of my mother my love for painting died as well."

* * * *

It had been three days since the attack on Theleshara and only one day since my mother and sister's funerals. I had learned that they would never wake again once their resting beds were lowered into the earth and covered in dirt.

Once again I found myself standing before the door that led into the painting room. The room that my mother and I would spend many hours together creating art. As I thought of these memories I could almost hear my mother's joyous laughter echoing from inside the room. My tiny hand rested upon the white wooden door. Each time I wondered down this hallway I found myself before this room, too scared to enter.

Just three days ago was my ninth birthday. Just three days ago my mother and I painted in this very room on the morning of my birthday. Together we worked on a massive canvas piece. Finally, I had worked up enough courage to enter the room. My small hand gripped the golden knob and turned it, the door creaked open as I pushed it. The afternoon sunlight filtered through the windows, bathing the room in a heavenly glow. My eyes wondered around the room, gazing upon the paintings that hung upon the walls and rested upon several easels that were scattered throughout the room.

My gaze landed upon a massive canvas that sat in the center of the room with two chairs seated before it. Hesitantly, I approached the unfinished painting. Palettes filled with dried paint and brushes rested upon the cushions of the chairs. Upon the canvas was painted many things; Theleshara's castle, the queen and her Pegasus, Estel, Renier, my mother, sister, and I. We all stood before the massive building with smiles upon our faces. Since my mother and I's painting style was exactly the same, the picture seemed as though it had been painted by one person.

My tiny fingers brushed against the dried paint and rested upon my mother and sister. They appeared so life-like, like they were about to walk out of the painting. Their smiling faces stared upon me. I couldn't bear to look upon them any longer. In the far corner of the room rested a blank canvas, I grabbed some paint and a brush and made my way toward the canvas. Pulling a chair with me I seated myself before the easel. I poured some paint into a clean pallet and dipped my brush into the fresh paint. Holding the brush before the canvas all I could do was stare at the blankness of it. I couldn't bring myself to place the brush upon it. I shook my head vigorously and tossed the brush across the room, red paint splattered upon the marble wall. I held my head in my hands as I cried out for my mother and sister.

* * * *

My memories burned brightly in my mind. This would be the first time that I speak to Haimera about my past.

"I-I'm so sorry Arendella. I did not know that." Guilt formed within her emerald eyes.

I smiled reassuringly to her, "It's okay. I feel as though it was about time I told you of my past. I know you have been curious about it and it's only fair I tell you of mine since you told me of yours." It' time for me to open up to her, to other people.

"Arendella, you do not have to tell me if you do not want too." She placed her hand over mine.

"On my ninth birthday King Andakile invaded Theleshara. My mother and sister fought against him but they were no match for the king. My sister was the first killed then my mother died protecting me." As I spoke of that day I found that I no longer cried. I had moved on from the pain, no longer did I blame myself for their deaths.

I knew it meant a lot to Haimera for me to open up to her. I trusted her and loved her as a sister. "I couldn't imagine what that must have been like for you at such a young age. A child shouldn't have to bear such pain." Tears glistened within her eyes and she grasped my hand.

"Just like you, I lost my mother at a young age. She was a fierce warrior, one of the best. But one day during a battle between the city wolves and forest wolves she was murdered." She sighed. "We Cyfasin people have a barbaric way of settling disagreements. And I lost my mother because the forest wolves refused to stop stealing food from the market." She laughed. "A stupid reason to die. At least she went down a warrior, a warrior that shall be spoken about for years to come."

Each of us have lost a mother, all in different ways were they taken from us. The women that bared us and birthed us into this world. The women that loved us. Though our stories and lives were different, we shared many similarities. Each of us were strong warriors, strong women, we each had our own important roles. And together we shall end this war.

"Every time we try to move away from sad subjects we find ourselves talking of something even sadder than the last." Crescent said.

I placed my hand on her shoulder, "Just shows that we trust one another to reveal our vulnerable sides."

A smile tugged at her lips. Today I knew I had gained another life-long friend. A knocking upon my door snapped our attention away from one another. One of the castle's servants popped her head into the room, "Queen Lyanthian asked for me to inform you that dinner shall be ready in five minutes."

I nodded my head to the woman, she smiled and closed the door once more. Turning my attention back to the two women sat before me, "Who's ready for some food?"

"I thought you'd never ask." Crescent playfully winked an auburn eye at me and jumped off the bed.

Haimera and I both exchanged giggled laughter as we followed the hungry Cyfasin princess down the hall and to the dining room. Soon the smell of freshly baked foods filled our nostrils. My mouth watered at the delicious scent, my stomach growled for the food. As we entered into the dining hall we saw that food lined down the middle of the table. A massive roast boar set in the center with several different vegetables circling around it. The enticing scent of cooked meat drew me to the table. Once we were all seated servants came around filling our glasses with white wine. Though, I did not favor this type of wine I knew the Cyfasin people did. It was one of their best goods for trade and they made it proudly.

"Lone Claw, what supplies and food are you requesting?" The elven queen questioned.

He took a sip of wine before speaking. "Wood for rebuilding homes and stores. Bread and vegetables to give out to the people, we can hunt our own meats. Medical herbs if you don't mind sparring some for us."

"All your requests shall be granted. I'll start having things packed onto some horses for your journey back home." Lyanthian clapped her hands together twice summoning a servant.

"Yes your majesty?" The brown haired elf servant came rushing from the kitchen.

"Please, get two horses from the stables and a wagon. Put as much wood, bread, vegetables, and healing herbs as you can into the wagon. Have it prepared by the time they are ready to leave."

"Yes your majesty." The girl bowed and hurried back into the kitchen.

"You are too generous, Lyanthian. Cyfaserin thanks you." Lone Claw raised his glass to the queen.

After dinner Crescent and Lone Claw saddled up their horses, thanked the queen one last time and departed Theleshara. Hopefully their supplies would last them long enough until they can start back their trades with the other kingdoms. But with Menanor still recovering as well, that being their number one trading partner, I knew that the Cyfasin people would rely more on Eshabel and us. Hopefully, we could still supply them with the food and things they need but I fear that if the war doesn't end soon, then we shall be needing supplies soon as well and cutting off our generosity. Hopefully, it won't come to that.

FESTIVAL OF THE FAE
CHAPTER 15

The following morning Queen Lyanthian had summoned Estel, Haimera, and I to the throne room. There she waited for us sitting upon her crystal throne, she stood when I entered and there within her dainty hands she held a letter. The seal upon it had been broken, meaning she had already read the contents inside. Once I was standing between Haimera and Estel she greeted me with a nod of her head.

"I have summoned you here because Queen Titiana has sent us an invitation to attend the *Festival of the Fae*." She paused and peered down at the letter, "Though I do not think it wise to leave Theleshara in such a dangerous time but Titiana highly insisted that we join her."

We stood in silence waiting for her to finish her thoughts on the matter. Her hazel eyes glanced over us and she continued once more.

"The king is no fool, he wouldn't attack us now for he must call forth more creatures for his army. And even he must rest, even with the power of the seals he is still human, mortal and must allow his body to recover, this he knows." She sighed. She had put some thought into this. "Still if an attack were to happen, I have left Uthtor in charge while we are gone. Soldiers will be stationed around the kingdom and rotated regularly. If anything were to happen Uthtor is to send me a message as soon as something occurs."

"So this means we are to join their festival?" Haimera asked excitedly. She loved parties.

"Yes." Lyanthian answered her.

"Oh I cannot wait! It'll take me all day to choose the perfect dress!" She exclaimed.

"Titiana has said not to worry with that, she shall have all of that taken care of." Queen Lyanthian began to descend down the marble stairs from her throne, "We shall leave in two hours, the festivities began at night fall."

It was still early morning, we would get there in time. Excitement bubbled inside me.

*   *   *   *

The horses were saddled up and waiting for us at the gates. Only our group of four was journeying to Eshabel. Queen Lyanthian opened the gates and led us out of the kingdom. We followed just behind her and arrived at Eshabel as the sun was barley sinking under the horizon. Soon the fae guards allowed us entrance into the kingdom and led our horses toward the castle. Once we were dismounted they then took the horses to the stables where they would wait for us until the festival was over.

Soon enough the fairy queen burst out of her castle with a bright smile upon her beautiful face. She approached our gathered group with a few fae men and women trailing behind her.

"I am so glad you have decided to join us! I know it is risky to be away from your kingdom but I wished for you to be a part of our festival, you haven't been a part of it for some time Lyanthian."

"It has been a long time. I fear though that this shall be the last time I might be able to join you." A painful look was written across her face.

Queen Titiana placed her hand upon the elven queen's shoulder, "Let us not speak of such sadness. Let us flourish in happiness." She clapped her hands and the group of men and women fluttered toward us. "My people shall help ready you for tonight." With that the queen returned to her castle. Estel was dragged away by two fae men while four fae girls led us toward the forest.

Soon we came upon a spring pool with a small waterfall that was decorated in vines and flowers of many colors. The plants grew beautifully around the pool. Rocks that surrounded the pool were smooth to the touch and colorful. Steam rose from the water. The sound of rushing water filled my ears as it crashed down upon the rocks from the waterfall. Flower petals floated atop the pool's surface, an aroma of flowery scent filled the air. Vines hung overhead with bulbs of not yet blossomed flowers growing from them. Wee pixies danced across the surface of the water but fluttered into the air when we approached.

The fae girls that led us here began to remove their clothes and entered into the spring pool, beckoning for us to join them. Haimera was the first of us to hop into the water soon followed by Queen Lyanthian. I was hesitant at first but soon gave in, I was with women. I had nothing to be ashamed of. The girls began to wash our hair, gently combing through our locks with wooden combs infused with the nectar from flowers. Then they began to scrub our bodies with sweet smelling oils. Soon the air around us smelt of flowers and sweets. Giggles then surrounded us, glittering specks fell before my eyes. I gazed up to see pixies dancing overhead.

"You'll have to forgive them, they are excited for the festivities." One of the fae girls chuckled as she finished combing Haimera's onyx hair.

We then sat in the spring, allowing the warm water to soften our skin and aching muscles.

"What exactly is the *Festival of the Fae*?" Haimera asked curiously.

A fae girl with shoulder length, purple hair answered her question, "It is celebrating a way of life should I say. Rebirth, the newness that spring brings, that being why we celebrate it within the first week of spring. We celebrate our magic, the nature around us, *The Great Oak of Life*." She pushed back her purple bangs that were cut to cover over one of her eyes. Her gaze was as lilac as the strands in my hair. Streaks of pink shot through her irises like lighting.

"And what do you do at the festival?" Haimera asked the girl.

"You shall see." She winked and stood from the pool.

Once our bodies were dry the fae girls handed us each a dress. The dresses complimented each of us in a unique way. Haimera's was tailored to fit low at the breasts and hung low on her shoulders with sleeves that flowed down to her hands. It was tightly fitted around her stomach and free flowing from her waist to the ground. It was a faded light green color, with brown detailing. The intricate details were woven in such an intricate way, the brown did not over power the light green color of the dress but instead it worked with it, making perfect harmony.

Instead of gifting her shoes, the fae girls gave to her foot jewelry. The golden anklets wrapped around her ankles and stopped just below her knees delicately.

Then the group of pixie fell from the sky and began to decorate Haimera's long wavy hair. They pulled a portion of her hair back, on both sides of her face, behind her shortly pointed ears and wove the hair into a braid. Letting the underneath of her hair remain untouched. Then two pixies lowered a small tiara fashioned from thin branches, decorated with white flowers, upon her head.

Next, was Queen Lyanthian. She was gifted with a dress that was pure white and silky to the touch. The hem of the dress was decorated with golden fabric. The dress tied behind the queen's neck, a golden circlet clasped the fabric just above her breasts, almost exposing them. Her pale shoulders and arms were left exposed. A golden strap was tied around her waist. The dress flowed to the ground delicately, creating a silky golden pool of fabric at her feet. When she turned around I saw that the back of the dress was open and stopped just at her lower back. She too was gifted with foot jewelry.

Once more the pixies dropped from the sky and began to decorate the queen's hair. They parted her honey golden hair down the center of her head, brushing some of the hair behind her long pointed ears, but leaving a thick strand of hair on either side to frame her face. Then they began to dance around in her hair, weaving thin braids throughout her golden locks. Then two pixies began to lower a tiara upon her head crafted from thin, white tree branches. A quartz crystal was woven into the tiara, it rested perfectly upon her head, the crystal aligning just in the center of her forehead.

Finally, it was my turn. The purple haired fairy gifted me with an amethyst colored dress. The fabric was shimmery and soft to the touch. There were no sleeves to this dress instead it held tight to my breasts. The fabric then turned into dark purple colored leather at my stomach, it crossed into the shape of an X, exposing my sides and a small portion of my stomach. The bottom of the dress returned to soft fabric and had a slit that ran up to my thigh. The fae girl gifted me with silver jewelry that wrapped up to my knees and gave me a silver bracelet that clasped around my exposed thigh.

The pixies swooped in and began to dress my hair. They let my hair fall into waves only putting a few small braids scattered throughout my long hair. Instead of placing a tiara upon my head they slid silver ear cuffs over my long pointed ears. Three thin chains hung from the edge of the cuffs and at the end of them hung small quartz crystals.

Once we were dressed the four fae girls led us back into the village were everything had been decorated within the time we were in the forest. Strands of lanterns hung across the stone streets, they were connected to the cottage homes and stores. Flower petals rained down from the sky; white, pink, and red colored petals scattered across the streets. Random fairies walked along the streets playing instruments and filling the air with music. Many carried flutes, harps, or sang songs of rebirth.

> *Oh let the great old oak grant us with new life,*
>   *Let the great old oak grant us with a promise of rebirth.*
>   *A promise of no more sorrow or pain.*
>   *Oh, let us flourish in the life we were gifted,*
>   *May we never take for granted what the great old oak has given,*

To us.

    The fae woman's voice was hauntingly beautiful, she carried out the last notes of song letting her voice ring through the air. Her small hand was placed upon her chest while her eyes were closed. Her blonde curly hair bounced as she swayed to her own song. Her creamy colored dress rode along the wind behind her, her golden wings fluttered softly sending glittering trails throughout the air around her. Pixies danced around her listening to her beautiful song.
    Soon we spotted the two fae men escorting Estel. Our groups soon met. Estel was dressed in a dark blue tunic and trousers. A black belt with silver embroidery was clasped around his waist. Black leather boots stopped just at his knees. Part of his hair was pulled back into a small braid while the rest fell to his shoulders. My heart raced at the sight of him. He was gorgeous.
    His ocean gaze washed over me. A smile tugged at his perfect lips. Slowly he approached me. My heart beat harder and harder the closer he came. Soon he stood before me.
    "Breathtaking." His lips whispered.
    The purple haired fae cleared her throat drawing our attention to her. "I'm sorry to interrupt but we are running a bit late."
    "My apologies." Estel placed his hand upon my lower back.
    The fae girl then continued to lead us toward the center of the town. An archway of flowers stood before us that led into the center of the town. A great deal had been put into this festival, and the festivities had yet to begin. Groups of two entered under the archway, the four fae girls broke into pairs and clasped each other's hands as they stepped under the archway. Then the two fae men were next. They peered lovingly into one another's eyes, clasped each other's hands and entered into the center of the town. Then it was Haimera, Queen Lyanthian, Estel, and I. I began to make my way toward the queen but Haimera swooped in front of her.
    "May I have the honor of escorting the queen?" She said extending a hand toward Lyanthian with a playful grin written upon her lips.
    "Of course." The queen giggled and took Haimera's hand in hers.
    When they passed us they both gave me a playful wink and walked under the archway giggling. Estel approached me and extended his hand to me. I gazed into his eyes and a smile formed on his lips. I slipped my hand in his and together we walked under the archway of flowers.
    The town square was filled with dancing fairies. Laughter and music filled the air. More lanterns hung over us, lighting the night in a golden glow. A group of fae sat in the center of the square playing their instruments. The sound of flutes and harps filled my ears with beautiful notes of harmony. Claps rang out around us and people began to partner up and took to the sky. Dancing in the night's darkness, dancing amongst the stars. Couples spun around one another, their wings fluttering with delight raining glittering specks upon the earth. Then they split into two lines and soon Queen Titiana appeared. She adorned a beautiful outfit that complimented her figure well. A white cloth wrapped around her breasts, a fiery red ribbon tied the top around the back of her neck, the ribbon crossed over itself across her chest creating an X shape. Her skirt was flowy with a spilt that raced up her thigh exposing her leg. The fabric of the skirts overlapped each other creating the puffiness of the skirt. Red ribbon tied low at her waist holding the skirt in place. A thin silver chain was connected to her top and three loops of silver chains hung from it upon her exposed belly, ruby crystals hung from the chains upon her

summery skin.

Upon her head rested a crown crafted from white branches with a large ruby at its center. Her fiery hair was woven into braids. One thick, long braid ran down the length of her back and two thinner braids fell from either side of her face and rested upon her breasts. She fluttered through the lines of her people and once she stood in the center of the town her people glided down from the sky and stood before their queen. Estel led me forward toward the gathered people, Haimera led Lyanthian as well. When we met Queen Titiana raised her hand in the air and her people fell to one knee before her, we did as well.

"We are here to celebrate life, rebirth, and *The Great Oak of Life*. We are here to give our thanks and also our sorrows. Sorrow for the lives that chose not to rejoin us and chose to remain with the tree, becoming one of the crystals to hang upon its branches. Thanks for the *Great Oak* allowing us to live once more, granting us with a new life." As she spoke her hair began to glow and small, fiery embers seemed to fall from her locks.

When I peered around me I noticed that the other fae people's hair began to glow as well. Those with green colored hair seemed to have small leaves sprouting and falling from the ends of their hair. Pink and purple haired fae had flower petals falling from their locks. Blue haired fae had water droplets cascading down their hair, creating puddles beneath them. Golden haired fae had glittering light raining down from their locks. The ends of the white haired fae seemed to become transparent and hovered through the air around them. Red and orange hair did the same as Titiana's.

Queen Lyanthian nudged me with her elbow, "The fair folk are close to nature, to the *Great Oak*. That is where they draw their magic from. They are created in many ways; blossomed from flowers, grown from a tree, created by rays of light, formed from a crystal, born from a wisp of wind, or from a small water droplet." She watched me staring upon the fairies magical hair.

"I thought they came from the tree?"

"The *Great Oak of Life* is the father of all the plants and nature that surround this kingdom. The tree chooses how the fae are created and when. If they die their souls return to it and the tree grants them with life once more, if the soul so chooses to live another life."

"So, the color of their hair shows what part of nature they were born from?" I asked.

"Yes, my dear child." It wasn't Lyanthian to answer me. I peered up to meet the fairy queen's golden gaze. She reached her hand out to me with a smile upon her lips. "Rise, child."

Queen Lyanthian shot a warning gaze to the fae queen. I looked upon her with curious eyes but Titiana drew me away from Lyanthian. She walked with regal demeanor as we walked around the town square. Many fae danced around us happily filling the air with their sounds of joyous laughter.

"You can venture a guess as to which part of nature I was born from."

I gazed upon her fiery hair, golden eyes, and wings. Her wings seemed like they had been torn at the ends, they reminded me of flames dancing from a log with how they pointed and waved. "Fire?"

"Yes. The destructive force of nature. Years before I became queen I feared myself and even many of the fae feared me." She sighed, "Not many fairies are born from the embers of fire, it is very rare. It took me years to learn how to control my magic and not to fear myself, that I wasn't just a force of destruction."

She chuckled and gazed upon me with a look that a mother would give her daughter. Her slender fingers brushed through my white-lilac hair. "But there are some that are even more rare, some that are born from…"

Queen Titiana stopped abruptly and met Queen Lyanthian's warning gaze. The queen released her hold on my hand, nodded to the elven queen, and made her way around the square. Queen Lyanthian followed after her. I tried to follow after the two queens but a strong hand gripped mine. I whirled around to meet the eyes of Estel. He brought my body close to his, his hand rested on the lower of my back sending a rush of heat through my body. Staring into his ocean eyes made it seem like the whole world fell away. That it was only us, here and now. The sounds of music and laughter faded away and soon all I could hear was our breathing and heart beats. I focused on his touch, the way his golden hair fell across his shoulders, the way his blue eyes filled with passion. His perfect lips twitched into a smile revealing his pearly white teeth. My hand slid up his chest, his neck, and rested upon his cheek. My thumb glided across his smooth skin. Slowly, I brought my lips to meet his. The softness of his lips felt so right against mine, so perfect. The taste of him filled my mouth and I craved more.

Slowly, Estel pulled his lips away from mine, breaking the kiss. His hand rested upon my cheek and his thumb gently traced over my bottom lip. There was so much sorrow buried deep within his eyes, so much fear.

"What troubles you?"

"The thought of losing you. I wish for you to stay out of the coming battle."

"I cannot, this you know. I shall not die so there is no need to fear, my love." I tried to reassure him with my words but they did not seem to ease his mind.

My hand was still rested upon his cheek, he grasped it and placed a tender kiss in the palm of my hand. "Fear always dwells within my mind."

Suddenly, the music grew louder and the fae began to dance around the town square. Dancing happily through the air or upon the ground. As usual I spotted Haimera in the center, dancing along to the rhythm of the fae's songs. Estel followed my gaze and led me toward the center of the town square. He bowed before me, extending his hand. "May I have the pleasure of a dance?"

Memories of my birthday flashed before my eyes. I couldn't help but think how much things have changed since then. "You may."

Just like the day of my birthday he placed his hand on the lower of my back and held my hand in his free one. We danced around the square, following the rhythm of the music. Allowing the music to lead and sway our bodies. Estel twirled me around like a princess and would bring my body back to his. His hands gripped my waist as mine rested themselves on the back of his neck, running my fingers through his hair. A blue feathered mask flashed in my mind, placing it upon his face. On that night Estel confessed his love for me but I had run away from him because I feared loved, but now I embrace it. Allowing myself to immerse in the love of another. I rested my head upon his chest, counting his heartbeats. For a while we danced in silence, the music filling the air around us. Slowly swaying our bodies together.

A green haired fae man tapped upon Estel's shoulder. Estel glanced behind him to meet the eyes of Fiori. The fae man smiled, "Sorry to intterupt but I wanted to ask Arendella if I may have a dance with her." His emerald eyes slid down my body, taking me in. "She looks absolutely stunning tonight."

Instead of allowing me to answer Estel pulled me closer to him. "Sorry but she has a dance partner, for the remainder of the evening." The elf gave the fae a warning glare.

"Why not let the lady speak for herself? Maybe she wishes to dance within the sky with a fae."

"I thank you for your offer but I am sorry to say that I must decline." I said to him.

"Ah, it is alright. No need for an apology." He grasped my hand and brought it to his lips and placed a tender kiss upon my skin. "May your evening be filled with joy and happiness, Arendella." He winked an emerald eye at me and disappeared into the sky.

The music slowly began to fade away and the air was filled with silence. Queen Titiana hovered in the sky above the fae that were once playing music. "My people, it is time for us to grant the *Great Oak of Life* with a visit. Rise and follow me into the forest where we shall bestow our thanks to the tree." She turned her golden gaze upon our small group of elves. "Queen Lyanthian, you and your people must remain here." Saying this she cut a sideward glance at me and then turned her back and disappeared into the forest, with her people following just behind her.

*   *   *   *

I lowered to the ground before the tree, my feet landing upon the plush, soft grass. Without turning to face my people I began to speak, "Now, will a fae from each element of nature step forth and grant a gift for the tree."

Footsteps sounded behind me and soon six fae stood beside me. Fiori, the fae man born from a tree leaf stood beside me. Allekai, the fae girl with short purple hair born from the petal of a flower stood beside Fiori. Leori, born from the first rays of sunlight on the first day of spring joined me by my side, his presence emanated with a sunny glow. Tetreara, the fae girl born from the smallest drop of rain stood beside Leori. Izabella, a young fae girl born from the currents of the wind took her place before the tree. Untorio, the last of my people to step forward, the last form of nature, he was born from a crystal.

Each of us stood before the *Great Oak of Life*, with outstretched hands we conjured forth our magic, presenting the tree with a gift from each of our elements of nature. Upon the outstretched palm of Fiori grew a tree leaf, upon Allekai's palm sprouted a purple flower, Leori conjured forth a radiant sphere of golden light, Tetreara summoned forth a mass of water that hovered over the palm of her hand, upon Untorio's palm formed a clear crystal, Izabella summoned forth a small tornado upon the palm of her hand, and finally I summoned forth a small flame. I remember when I first did this, I feared that my magic would burn the tree but I soon realized that it would not harm it.

I nodded my head to my people and slowly we sent our gifts toward the tree, each of the elements of nature hovered toward it. The center of the tree slowly opened and golden light flooded onto the land, each of the elements infused into the tree, making the crystal leaves upon its branches glow brightly as it accepted our gifts.

As the crystals glowed I peered around and saw that my people's hair and wings glowed in response to the tree. Glittering trails whirled around within the air from the fluttering wings of the fae. In unison my people and I began to sing for the *Great Oak of Life*. Our voices synched in perfect harmony. The men taking on the low notes while the women sang the higher ones.

> *Oh let the great old oak grant us with new life,*
>   *Let the great old oak grant us with a promise of rebirth.*
>   *A promise of no more sorrow or pain.*
>   *Oh, let us flourish in the life we were gifted,*
>   *May we never take for granted what the great old oak has given,*
>   *To us.*
>   *We shall be ever grateful and cherish this precious gift of life.*
>   *May we always give a gift of magic back to the tree.*
>   *And may the Great Old Oak watch over us from now,*
>   *Until the end of time.*

Our voices drifted along the currents of the wind, carrying our melodies across the land. Soon, silence surrounded us as we bowed our goodbyes and left the forest, returning to the town square.

   *   *   *   *

Fae filled the night sky, some fluttered down to the town square to continue the festivities while the rest retired to their homes for the night. Queen Titiana approached our group.

"Is visiting the tree the main part of the festival?" I asked.

"Yes. Each year we give the tree our thanks and gift to it presents from each form of nature."

"Why do you do so?" Curiosity ate at me.

"The tree grants us with life and magic, keeps us alive. Wouldn't you want to give someone your thanks if they brought you into this world and bestowed upon you magic?"

"I would want to repay them for the life they had given to me." Saying this my heart ached. My hand clenched itself over my chest as I thought of my mother. She brought me into this world and I couldn't save her.

Queen Titiana's golden eyes stared into my face, "Something troubles you?"

"No, just exhausted is all."

"Ah, it is rather late into the night and you still have to travel back to Theleshara." She peered over her shoulder and called forth the purple haired fae girl from earlier today before the festival. "Tetreara, take them to castle so that they may change back into their own clothes for their journey back home."

Tetreara led us back to the fae queen's castle and into one of the rooms on the second floor, Estel had been led to another room so that he may change. Tetreara left us to retire to her room for the night.

"Before we leave I need to use the ladies room, that wine is starting to get to me." Haimera said before dashing from the room and down the hall. Queen Lyanthian and I exchanged a few laughs while we listened to Haimera's hurried footsteps.

"So, Arendella, did you enjoy yourself tonight?" Lyanthian asked me.

"Very much. I enjoyed the music and dancing and even the bath before the festival."

The queen smiled warmly and brushed some hair behind my ear. "We all needed this. Everything has been so saddening lately, I'm glad I decided to accept Titiana's invitation."

"It was a much needed break I should say." I chuckled as I slipped on my boots.

"How are things with you and Estel?" Her question caught me off guard.

"Great, why do you ask?"

"I watched you two dance together earlier. The loving way you peered at one another made me happy."

I cocked my head to the side, "Why?"

"Because, you are finally letting people close to you, letting them love you. Not only have you let Estel get close to you, you have also allowed Haimera too." Her hands rested upon my shoulders. "It makes me more than happy to see you open up to people, to see you embrace love once more. I'm glad you are no longer allowing what happened so long ago to hold you back anymore. You are moving on."

"I'll never move on, Lyanthian, It is still pain that I must deal with every day and something that haunts me every night." I peered into her hazel eyes, "You too deal with pain, a pain so similar to mine. And you as well have not moved on from it."

"You are right but we cannot allow our pain to define us or hold us back. We must accept it and move forward with our lives. My husband, my king, is still in my thoughts and held within my heart every day, there he shall stay for the remainder of my life." Her hand rested upon my chest over my heart, "And in here is where your mother and sister are. They are with you always."

The door to the room was opened and in staggered Haimera, she leaned against the wall seeming sickly. "I do say that fae wine is *very* strong. Please, next time remind me not to drink so much."

"Will you be okay for the journey home?" Queen Lyanthian asked her.

"Of course. I just feel sorry for the poor horse I shall be riding. Poor thing has to deal with my sickened drunk self."

A little while later, when Haimera had some time to rest, we gathered in front of the castle. Our horses were brought to the front of the castle led here by two fae men, each one holding a set of reins in each hand guiding our four horses toward us. Queen Titiana descended down the marble steps of the castle and approached us.

"May your travels be safe and you return home good and well."

"We thank you for your invitation Titiana. I shall send you a message as soon as we arrive at Theleshara."

THE TRUTH MUST COME OUT
CHAPTER 16

"Titiana, I've told you my thoughts on this. There must be another way." Lyanthain paced along the emerald green carpet within my castle.

"Lyanthian, the king is coming for Theleshara's seal next. He is now too powerful for either of us to fight. But Arendella might stand a chance against him if you allow me to awaken every bit of untapped power that is locked away inside her."

"It's too much of a risk that I'm not willing to take. That power could destroy her and the land of Lylanalian."

"The king is going to destroy this land and Arendella is our chance to save it. Lyanthian, you know this deep within your heart. Why else would you come here seeking my help if you knew what I was to say?" My eyes watched the elven queen as she paced about the room uneasily, sorting through her thoughts. Her eyebrows knitted together causing her forehead to crease.

"I fear for the child. I fear of how this shall affect her. I thought hiding the truth from her would keep her safe but fate has decided otherwise."

"The truth must always come out. This you know."

The queen's shoulders slumped with heavy burden. Her mind flowing with worry.

"Andakile is preparing his army. I cannot predict when he shall march to my kingdom but every minute I waste is another minute he's gained."

"It seems to me that you have decided."

Her hazel eyes met with mine, and in them I found defeat, worry, despair. "I have no other choice do I?"

"We always have a choice, Lyanthian." I rose from my throne and approached her. "But the question is, was it really your choice to hide from Arendella the truth? Or is it her choice to find out who she truly is? I know the child is curious about her life, parents, and heritage."

"I vowed to her mother that I would keep Arendella safe and I thought that meant hiding the truth from her. But now I realize that I was wrong."

I grasped the elven queen's hands. "You did what you thought was best and I do not blame you for that."

Her gaze met with mine and regret was now reflected in her hazel eyes. "I am truly sorry for the words I had spoken to you. I should never have threatened to move you or your people from my kingdom."

My arms embraced the queen and I breathed in her summery scent. "You have always been like a sister to me and I forgive you. I forgave you on that day because I knew you were only trying to protect the girl."

She returned the embrace. "When would you like to speak with Arendella?"

I stepped back from the queen and returned to my throne. "The sooner the better. We don't have much time left." I said as my fingers traced along the leaf pattern carved into the white wood of my throne.

"I'll send her to you as soon as I return to Theleshara, you may tell her and teach her whatever you wish. I am leaving her in your hands now. Take care of my daughter for me." Though Lyanthian knew Arendella wasn't her daughter by blood she accepted her as one. The queen's love for the child was that of any other mother; undying and loyal.

"I swear upon my life to keep her safe. You have my word." I placed my hand upon my heart swearing an oath.

Once the queen had left the castle, the wooden doors shutting behind her, I stood from my throne and exited the castle. I stood upon the top stair watching Lyanthian depart. Her honey golden hair shone in the moonlight and her wavy locks flowed along the wind. The pearl silk of her dress rippled through the air behind her as she approached the golden gates of my kingdom. One of my guards allowed her out. She peered over her shoulder and left. The golden gates slowly closing behind her.

Soon, Arendella would arrive and she would finally know who she truly is.

And the king would be brought down.

A NOTE
CHAPTER 17

Queen Lyanthian had disappeared from the castle without word of where she was going. The guards and servants had no idea as to where she went. Not even a note was left behind detailing when she would return. She left the day after we returned from Eshabel. I had only hoped she would come back in time before the king arrives. My stomach sank with a feeling that we would lose this battle, just like the others. Now our chances were near zero. With the power of four seals none of us truly stood a chance against him. The four of us against one man didn't stand a chance. But would a whole army?

As I leaned upon the railing of my balcony my eyes watched Uthtor's training soldiers. Haimera and I have been waking every morning and training every day until late in the afternoon. Though I've trained before I have never trained as hard as I do with Haimera. Today our training ended early, before lunch giving me time to relax and ease my mind. Though I wished to spend this time with Estel, I couldn't. He was down there with Uthtor training soldiers. I watched the back of his golden head until he turned and looked up to my balcony. His ocean blue eyes met with mine. A smile tugged at his lips. He waved to me and returned to his training.

*   *   *   *

"No, you promised me you would leave her out of this!" I yelled at the mirror, pulling at my hair.

"You can no longer defy me, Renier. I told you that I wouldn't touch the girl and I told you that I would gladly hand her over to you once I have complete control over Lylanalian."

"But why must she be involved in this plan?"

The king's chuckle echoed from the mirror. "I need her away from the castle. All you must do is slip her a note underneath her door and your role in this plan shall be done."

I shook my head vigorously. "No! No! No!" I fell to my knees clasping my hands over my ears. The voices wouldn't leave me alone. They kept telling me to do such horrible things. "Get out of my mind!" I screamed.

"I told you that you can no longer defy me. You must do everything that I ask of you."

"You're the one that made me treat Arendella in that way. You made me say and do things that I didn't want to do!" My arm began to throb in pain where he had marked me. My flesh was itching and burning. I clawed at it wanting to remove his mark from my skin. I clawed and clawed until my fingernails were covered in my own blood. And still the mark was there.

"Claw at it all you wish but it shall never come off. And I never made you do anything, that was your own deep desires forcing you to act in such a way, though I cannot say that my magic didn't play a role in that. It simply ignited the dark desires within you." He cackled loudly enjoying my suffering. "Now, rise and face me." As he commanded my body stood from the ground but not under my doing. He forced me to look him within those crimson eyes of his.

"You shall slip a note underneath her door tonight, detailing exactly where I want her. Understood?"

"Yes, your majesty."

"Good boy. Now I must finish preparing my soldiers." With that the mirror returned to its reflective surface and my own reflection was staring back at me. I fell to my knees once more.

I forced my body to stand from the floor. Seating myself at my desk I began to write the note. As the ink lined the paper my heart sank with each blackened letter.

Why is fate so cruel?

*   *   *   *

Word of the queen's return spread around the castle like wild fire. Once I heard of the news I made my way to the throne room. Upon entering the room, I found that quite a few people were gathered before the queen. Most of them were worried guards and servants asking her where she went and why she didn't leave a note informing them she was leaving. When the queen's hazel gaze fell upon me she stood from her throne and dismissed everyone from the room. They quickly filed out of the room leaving Lyanthian and I alone. I stepped toward her and bowed.

"Arendella, you have many questions that you wish to be answered. About your family and heritage. Though I shall not be the one to answer those questions."

"Then who is to tell me?"

"I'm sending you to Eshabel, there Titiana shall tell you everything you need to know."

My heart raced. "When do I leave?"

"Tomorrow morning."

I left the throne room with excitement bubbling inside me. Finally, I shall have all my questions answered and I'll know about my father.

I opened the door to my chamber expecting to find Estel waiting for me but he was nowhere to be found. He was possibly helping Uthtor so I thought nothing much of it. I approached my closet and picked out a night gown. I tossed the light pink dress upon the bed and began to undress. I had barely lifted my tunic over my head when a letter slipped inside my room from underneath my door. Fixing my shirt, I bent down and plucked the letter from the floor. My door creaked open and I peeked my head into the hallway to find no one. I shut the door and unfolded the letter.

Dear Arendella,

Meet me at the cliff that looks over the Thelarian Ocean at midnight.

Sincerely, Estel

    Excitement rushed through my being. I looked out into the night sky, the moon was almost at its highest point. It would soon be midnight. Finally, I could tell Estel my joyous news.

    *   *   *   *

    Once I had slipped the note beneath her door I rushed back to my chamber and locked myself inside. The voices kept whispering inside my mind. Singing their songs of torment. My fingers clawed at my ears, I wished to not hear the voices anymore. I wished for them to disappear. But they never stopped humming their tunes of despair. My body sank to the cold floor as tears wept from my eyes.
    I heard the sound of a door open and the sound of hurried footsteps echo down the hallway. It was midnight and Arendella was falling into the king's trap. A trap I had helped him set. My stomach twisted itself into a knot. This feeling I had overwhelmed my being. I refused to let her fall into his grasp once more. I forced my body to stand and ignored the voices in my mind. I thrust my door open and followed after Arendella.

    *   *   *   *

    Without knocking I entered into Renier's chamber. The freezing air crawled along my skin. My breath visible within the air. The room was dark except for the moonlight that crept inside through the holes in the curtains. Using my staff, I called upon a ball of flame to light the darkened chamber. Sheets of parchment were scattered amongst the stone floor. I knelt down to the floor and examined the papers, inked words danced across the surface. Words I couldn't understand. My eyes caught droplets of crimson that stained the floor. I followed the trail to a mirror that hung upon the wall. And there written across the surface, in fresh blood, was a symbol used to call upon someone whom was far away. Except this symbol was corrupt. I could feel a disturbance in the magic used upon the mirror. My stomach sank. I quickly left Renier's room and hurried to Arendella's. I thrust her door open to find that she was nowhere to be found. But setting upon a small table by the door was a letter. A letter used to lure her out of the castle. My heart raced and I hurried from the castle hoping to reach her in time.

FALLING INTO THE KING'S TRAP
CHAPTER 18

Once it was midnight I made my way through the castle and toward the gates. Placing my hand upon the cool silver my palm radiated a faint purple glow, slowly the gates opened and I made my way toward the Thelarian Ocean.

Soon the cliff was in sight and I hurriedly made my way up the steep side trying to reach the peak. Once I had reached the top my eyes landed upon a figure of a man standing at the very edge, the hood of his cloak was pulled over his head and his back was to me. I slowly approached him.

"Estel, why did you wish to meet me here?"

The man didn't answer me, didn't face me. I stopped in my tracks and watched the person carefully. Studying their movements. There was a feeling in my gut, an instinct to run. I began to back away from the man but he slowly turned to face me.

"Ah Arendella, what a pleasure it is to see you again." That cackling voice sent a chill down my spine. The man reached up and removed his hood, exposing his scar ridden face and blood red hair. His grey skin now had a tint of green to it, his crimson eyes the same as always; craving a thirst for blood.

"Andakile, I must say that it is never a pleasure to see you." My fist gripped my staff tightly in my hand. My palms beginning to sweat.

I could feel the evil magic pulsating off his aura. Corrupting the air around him.

"Why did you lure me here?" I demanded.

He chuckled and tossed his cloak over the edge of the cliff, watching it slowly fall into the ocean. "Because my dear Arendella, you have a bad habit of getting in my way. And I must break that habit." He advanced toward me with a malicious smile written upon his scared lips.

I braced myself for an attack. Fear rose inside my being. I couldn't fight him, not alone. Four of us didn't stand a chance against him. My body shook with fear. But I couldn't let doubt cloud my mind. I needed to focus on staying alive. Suddenly I felt a presence within my mind plucking and pulling on my memories.

Andakile's chuckle sounded in my head, "Ah, I see my Arendella isn't so pure anymore. Oh, you naughty girl. It's a shame I couldn't get a taste of you."

"You bastard stay out of my head!" Summoning upon my magic I called forth lighting.

It crackled within the air between us as it raced toward him. But as it inched closer to him, he smirked, and flicked his hand through the air. My lighting redirected and stormed into the sky.

"Simple magic won't defeat me." He unsheathed his sword, the metal hissed from its sheath. The blade radiated a faint crimson glow, wisps of red danced from the metal like flames. Every bit of him was cursed. His body, soul, and now any weapons he possessed was tainted with corrupt magic. He advanced toward me, slowly. Teasing me. Taunting me.

Chills ran along my spine. The arms on my hair stood on end. I grounded myself. Planting my feet firmly on the ground, I gripped my staff within my hands. Though I might not be strong enough to defeat him, I would damn well try with every fiber of my being to bring him down. His smirk only grew as he watched my face fill with determination.

The crystal atop my staff began to radiate a red light as I called forth flames. Instead of blazing streaks of fire I changed the form and summoned upon spheres of flames. They shot from the crystal repeatedly, one after the other. Andakile sliced his sword through the air, through the balls of flames that were targeted at him. He wasn't fast enough to slice every one, some slammed into his body, sending him staggering backward.

Simple magic my ass.

My heart ignited with hope. A flame of courage burned inside my being. I set forth another set of flames and then charged at him. While he was busy trying to dodge my magical attack I attacked him with the dagger end of my staff. The blade sliced through his right bicep, sending black tar gushing into the air and spraying across my face. The substance trickled down my staff.

"You have become such a pest! I should have killed you when I had the chance, I won't be making that mistake again!" He bellowed as he brought his sword down toward me. Quickly I evaded his attack as his blade sliced through the empty air where I once stood.

Quickly I called forth vines, they sprouted from the ground and wrapped themselves around the king's legs, rooting him in place. Once again I charged toward him, ready to pierce him through the heart and end his life. But before the dagger of my staff could enter his body his sword met with my staff. The sound of metal dancing against metal rang in the empty air around us. I jumped backward away from him, deciding that it would be safest to keep my distance. His sword whacked through the vines that held him and he was free of my magic.

"I sense a powerful magic inside you, Arendella. I remember how you escaped from my castle. No ordinary elf could have called forth magic without their staff." He waltzed toward me, his sword dragging along the dirt ground. "I shall cut you open and find out exactly what magic is locked away inside of you."

He gripped his sword with both hands and pointed it in my direction. The red aura pulsated off of it like flames. At the point of his sword a crimson light began to form in the shape of a sphere. Its size increased with each passing second. Quickly I called forth my magic. I stabbed the dagger end of my staff into the earth and summoned upon every ounce of magic I could. The crystal upon my staff lit up with the light of the moon. Andakile's sword sent a beam of cursed magic crackling through the air toward me. It had the form of crimson colored lighting. With a shout I sent a beam of holy light to meet with his. They slammed into one another. A blast of wind rushed my way from the force of our magic. The wind caused bits of sand and dirt to blind me for a mere few seconds.

Andakile's eyes grew darker and darker as he continued his attack. His lips cracked into a malicious smile. His magic was forcing mine back, his red beam growing dangerously close to me. I mustered up all the will power I had and forced my magic forward, pushing his beam back. Our magic lit up the dark night. Painting the air and earth around us in shades of red and white. Good and evil. Light and dark.

    My feet began to skid along the ground, upturning the earth beneath me. The only thing holding me in place was the dagger of my staff planted firmly in the ground, I kept ahold of my staff. Beads of sweat dripped down my brow and spine. My breathing was heavy. My body was growing tired but still I summoned upon my magic. I wouldn't stop until the king was dead. I would force myself to keep going. The more magic I called forth the more my body protested.

    Suddenly there was a burning sensation within the palms of my hands. My gaze locked upon my staff to see the crystal ball cracking. Thin lines shot through the crystal and my staff felt like it was on fire. Thin cracks began to race along the pole of the staff, dancing around the silver like lightning. Once my gaze locked with Andakile's my staff shattered. Pieces of the crystal burst into the air and reflexively I let go of the staff and shielded my eyes. I felt as the burning silver of my staff pierced my body, seeping into my skin. I felt the warm blood trickling down my body. Then there was an explosion of magic that sent my body flying into the sky, flying off the cliff and into the Thelarian Ocean. My body hit the water like stone, it ached from the force of the water. Stars twinkled before my eyes as I sank deeper into the depths of the ocean. Panic took over my being, I struggled to hold my breath but my body gasped for air. I breathed in the salty water. The bitterness of it washed down my throat, into my lungs. I fought hard against the current of the waves trying to swim to the surface but my body just couldn't fight any longer. So, I gave in to the ocean. I let my body sink deeper and deeper as my vision became nothing but darkness. I closed my eyes accepting my death.

    Then I felt a familiar inch in the palms of my hands. An inch and burn of magic. Through the darkness of the water I could see a faint glow of purple radiating from the palms of my hands. Using this magic, I was able to blast through the water, all the way to the surface. I breathed in air, swallowing it. My lungs filled with air once more. As I crawled onto the shore I coughed up large amounts of water. The salt caused my throat to dry and burn. My gaze locked with Andakile's as I stared up toward the cliff I had just fallen from. He appeared disappointed that I was still alive.

    Looking down at my palms I saw that they still radiated that purple light. A new magic was surging through my body. I felt powerful, more powerful than I did before. I stood from the ground and faced the king. My gaze locked with his. And in his eyes I saw a flicker of fear, a flicker of curiosity. I watched his lips whisper, *What are you?*

    My arms rose into the sky and as they did, large masses of waves rose into the sky behind me. They were mine to command. Mine to control. And I would use them to kill the king once and for all.

    Just as I was about to drag the king into the depths of the ocean I felt a piercing pain in my stomach. A pain so great I almost collapsed. My gaze wondered down to my stomach and there I saw a dagger embedded into my skin. Dark blood oozed from the wound and painted the sand beneath my feet in red. The waves crashed behind me and my gaze locked with Renier's.

    My body fell to the sandy ground. An immense pain took over me, blood poured out onto the sandy beach painting it in crimson. The dagger was still embedded into my stomach. My hand grasped around the hilt and pulled. A scream escaped me as the steel slowly left my body and I tossed the dagger aside. I pressed my hand against my stomach trying to stop the bleeding. But blood oozed between my fingers. Stars twinkled before my eyes as my vision wavered. I tried so hard to fight against death but this was a battle that I would not win. Slowly my eyes closed as I let out my last breath.

*   *   *   *

I watched as her body plummeted through the air. I watched as her white hair disappeared into the ocean. My heart sank, it shattered. I rushed to the ocean to save her but the king caught sight of me. His magic took hold of my being and my body was his to command. Fear then gripped my soul as I watched her emerge from the water. She crawled onto the shore, her white-lilac hair was tangled, her clothes drenched. Then she stood from the ground and faced the king. Her hands glowing purple. She summoned upon magic I had never seen nor felt before. As the waves rose into the sky my body began to march toward her and my hand took a dagger from a notch on my belt. I fought against his magic, trying to regain control over my body but nothing I did worked. So, I was forced to watch as my hand stabbed the dagger into Arendella's stomach. I felt the warmness of her blood on my skin. And then, her gaze met with mine as the water crashed behind her. A question lingered in her blue eyes; *why?* Tears prickled in my eyes as I watched her collapse to the ground. She struggled to fight against death but slowly she was losing that fight. Her eyes clouded over and I knew that life had slipped away from her. Finally, the king released his hold on me and I fell to my knees beside Arendella. Hot tears streamed down my face as I cried out in agony.

The girl I loved was dead and it was my fault.

*   *   *   *

"What have you done!" I cried out at Renier as I rushed toward Arendella.

Renier saw me and ran deep into the darkness of the night. My knees hit the wet, blood soaked, sand beside Arendella. I clutched her drenched body in my arms, pulling her onto my lap. Her stomach gushed with blood, a dagger lay upon the ground beside her. I brushed away the tangled wet hair from her face. Small trickles of blood escaped the corners of her blue-tinted lips. Her skin was ice cold. Her face pale. Her eyes lifeless. I cupped my hand around her cheek. My heart felt as though it were falling apart, piece by piece. My soul felt like it was being torn away from my body. My tears fell onto her face as I cried trying to heal her with my magic. But nothing worked. No amount of magic would bring my Arendella back to me. She was gone, forever. I hugged her body to mine, rocking back and forth as I cried out her name. Her blood stained my green tunic, painting it in her life force.

"My love, please don't leave me. You are my heart and soul. Come back to me, Arendella." My cries of sorrow echoed around me.

The sound of hurried footsteps approached me and Haimera fell to the ground beside me. Her hands dug into the red sand. Mortified, the halfling lifted her blood soaked hands and stared upon them. Droplets of blood fell from her fingers. Her emerald eyes widen in shook. Her head shook from side to side.

"No. She can't be. Tell me it isn't true!" Her cries of sorrow filled my ears. "Tell me she isn't dead!" Her fists pounded the sandy ground as she cried out louder.

A nod of my head gave her the answer she never wanted to know. Her fists clenched the wet, sandy ground. Her shoulders shook as she cried. The king had taken away from us the one person who meant more to us than our own lives. Our gazes then followed that of an army that marched its way toward Theleshara with Andakile leading his horde of Forgotten. There was nothing we could do to stop him, there were simply too many of his creatures. We were outnumbered and now Theleshara's seal would be destroyed.

THE FINAL SEAL
CHAPTER 19

"We need all of our soldiers at the front of the gates now!" I commanded Uthtor as I rushed from the castle and into the castle gardens. I heard Uthtor shout commands to his soldiers and the sound of rushing footsteps filled the air as soldiers marched toward the front of the kingdom. Women and children rushed around the castle into the forest to hide away from the approaching battle. The sound of an explosion rang in the air and the sounds of battle followed shortly after.

I stood before the garden fountain and stared into the clear water. In my heart, in my soul, I felt as though something happened. Though I couldn't tell what, I knew that when I found out it would break my heart.

The sounds of battle drew near. I turned to see my people being struck down by the king's army. Forgotten stabbed at my soldiers, my people, killing them mercilessly. Bodies littered the streets. Bodies of mothers and their children that didn't hide in time. Houses burned. Screams of chaos and agony filled the air. My heart ached as I listened to the sound of my people being slaughtered. But I couldn't leave to protect them. My place was here, to protect the final seal.

"Lyanthian, half of my soldiers are gone, the king shall be here any second. We must leave." Uthtor approached me.

"Make sure to get the survivors out of the kingdom, go to Eshabel you shall be safe there."

"You cannot stay here Lyanthian. It's over, he's won!"

"It's not over, not yet. I shall stay here and fight to protect this seal with my life."

"Then let me stay and help you."

"No, I need you to protect my people."

Suddenly, an ear-piercing roar rattled our eardrums. We looked to the sky and saw a giant mass of darkness flying above my kingdom. Blazing streaks of flames fell from the sky and set fire to everything that crossed the fire's path. Elves frantically ran about as flames ate at their bodies. Many of my people lay about the ground, slaughtered or burned.

Where was Arendella? She has the necklace to call upon Syllviona.

"Uthtor, have you seen Arendella?" I questioned the elven man.

"No, I heard some maids talking and they said that they saw her leave the castle some hours ago, but they don't know where she went. Renier, Estel, and Haimera are also gone."

Then the beast's crimson gaze locked with mine, once more it let out another ear-piercing roar and it plummeted from the sky. The earth shook beneath our feet as the dragon landed before us. Smoke escaped the dragon's nostrils. Its tongue flickered between its open jaws. My eyes wondered over to Uthtor, the bravest warrior and dearest friend I have come to know so well. He stood beside me, his fists clenching his wooden staff. His mahogany hair was tied back in a braid but tendrils of hair escaped from it. His clothes were tattered and a thin cut scared his right cheek, small blood droplets wept from the wound. I reached out and placed my hand upon his broad shoulder, "Go." I whispered to him, my gaze caught his. Concern sparked within his emerald eyes. I turned away from him and stood before the mighty dragon.

"It's been a long time, Thorodan."

Indeed it has, Lyanthian. His menacing voice echoed throughout my mind.

Footsteps approached me from behind, "Uthtor, I order you to leave. Now. Protect my people." And with those words he hurried off to save a family of elves from being slaughtered. Then a figure approached us. I could sense his evil aura spilling onto the land, corrupting the air around him. His blood red hair soared along the currents of the wind. His crimson eyes glowed brightly through the darkness. His sword dragged along the ground beside him as blood dripped from the blade. The blood of my people. My stomach turned to knots as I thought of the women, children, and men he slaughtered mercilessly.

"Lyanthian, you know why I'm here. Now, step aside." He pointed the tip of his sword at me as he waltzed toward me.

"I shall protect this seal with my life, Andakile, this you know." I readied myself for an attack. But I knew I was no match against him and Thorodan. In my mind I had accepted defeat but in my heart I refused to go down without a fight.

The dragon said nothing, never moved from his place. Just stood there watching me. Watching the king. "I wanted this to be a fight just between us, *Queen*." Andakile stated.

I summoned upon hundreds of years, worth of magic, it pulsated through my being, coursing through my veins. My body thrummed with power, a power I hadn't called forth in some time. My body ignited with strength. My staff reacted with the magic, the ruby crystal glowing brightly. My eyes met with Andakile's, and in his gaze I found no soul, no heart, nothing. All he desired was to quench his thirst for blood. He was a killing machine, a beast.

All beasts must be slain.

Suddenly, Thordan took flight and returned to the skies. His massive wings carried him away into the darkness of the night. His purpose here was done.

"Tell me, Andakile, how you convinced the dragon to aid you."

He chuckled as he shook his head from side to side, "Simple. We both crave destruction. Blood. Death. It proved to be very easy to convince Thorodan."

Dark masses of magic crept along the ground toward me. They slithered like serpents ready to attack. The ruby crystal upon my staff radiated a bright glow and I swept it through the dark masses, slicing them in half. But to my dismay they formed back and rose into the air.

Acting quickly, I summoned a protection barrier to keep Andakile away from the seal. A transparent dome formed itself around the seal and I. The king merrily chuckled and stepped toward the dome. He reached out his hand and poked his finger at the barrier. Suddenly a cloud of black and red mist formed and ate away at dome. It spread quickly engulfing it, I was surrounded by darkness. Then the sound of cracking rang around me and the dome shattered. Tiny flickers of magic fell around me and the cloud of mist was at my feet. Its touch chilled me to my bones. It wrapped itself around my legs, slowly crawling up my body. The mist seemed to whisper, words of torment filtered through my ears, singing its song of agony.

"Enough of this madness!" My voice caused a wave of magic to surge from my body, blasting away the king's magic. Its shrieks filled the night. "Enough of these games, Andakile."

"I was only trying to have a little fun, Lyanthian." He shrugged his shoulders and called back his mist. "I was trying to take it easy on you, women aren't as strong as men."

"Some of the best warriors in times past were women, need I remind you."

"Enough talk of this nonsense, I came here for one purpose. And I'll leave with the power I came here seeking." His eyes flashed a bright red, he was calling forth his magic once more.

He advanced toward me, slowly. I kept my position, I had to protect the seal no matter the cost. I would not let fear turn me into a coward, not this time. I have stayed away from battles for far too long, sending my children to fight for me. It's time for me to step up and be the queen my people need.

"As long as I'm still breathing, that power shall never be yours!"

A blast of magic shot forth from the ruby atop my staff. The golden ray of light aimed at the king. He smirked. Seeming as though he had nothing to fear, nothing to worry about. He acted like he could defeat me so easily. That I was no match for him. But he was wrong. I would prove to him that I was not someone who would be defeated so easily.

With one arm, he held his sword in front of him. The fiery looking mist that radiated from the steel crawled along the sword and began to form itself into a crimson sphere at the tip. It shot forth, crackling through the air like crazed lightning. His attack met with mine. Sparks of magic blasted through the air as our beams collided with one another. He was strong. Stronger than before. The seal's corrupt magic was giving him strength and power. With this final seal he could be unstoppable.

I felt a presence within my mind. It sorted through my memories, plucking and pulling at them. Digging deeper and deeper into my brain. The presence found itself within my childhood memories, my adult memories. It was everywhere. But what was it searching for?

Then it pulled forth a memory from so long ago that was still as heart breaking as it was on that day. "Andakile, stay out of my mind!"

"Oh, but this memory of yours is my favorite." Malicious cackles escaped him.

*   *   *   *

"Please, tell me where we are going?" A smile wore itself upon my lips as I gripped my lovers hand tightly. He had tied a scarf around my eyes and told me he had a surprise waiting for me.

"We are almost there my dear." His rich voice filled my ears.

Soon we came to a stop. He let go of my hand and moved to stand behind me. His arms circled around my waist and his hot breath trailed down my neck. "We are here." He removed the scarf and what I saw before me was the Thelarian Ocean, waves gently rolled onto the sandy shore. The sun was slowly sinking, painting the sky in brilliant colors of red and orange. A red blanket had been laid out and a basket sat on top of it.

"Maximus..." My lips whispered his name as he led me toward the picnic.

I seated myself upon the plush red fabric as he opened the basket and grabbed two wine glasses from it. He set one before me and began to pour my favorite wine into it. Its rich crimson color filled the clear glass. My eyes gazed upon the man that sat before me. His midnight dark hair was combed neatly to the side. His white tunic was loosely tied at the top exposing his manly chest, short black hairs peaked out from his shirt. His rich brown eyes finally met with mine. The sun shone into them, turning them into a bright auburn color with flecks of colored honey scattered throughout his irises. A smile tugged at his thin, moist lips allowing his pearly white teeth to show.

"What made you come up with this surprise?" I asked him.

"To show you how much I love you."

My heart had a fiery warmth spread throughout it. A warm feeling of love. This man, my husband, my king, has been married to me for almost twenty years and everyday he showers me with love. He makes sure that I know he appreciates me. And every day I fall more in love with him. Never in my hundreds of years did I think I would find my other half. But the gods have given this man to me and I would cherish him forever.

I scooted my body closer to his, seating myself in his lap. I stared upon his handsome face, my thumb traced over his bottom lip. His dark chin stumble rubbed against the palm of my hand. I brushed back some of his dark hair behind his pointed ear. His hands gripped my waist, pulling my body closer to his. We pressed against each other as we stared into one another's eyes. His fingers trailed along my spine, gently. Sending a rush of heat through my being.

Maximus leaned toward me and whispered into my ear, "Twenty years and I'm still as madly in love with you as I was the first time I lay my eyes upon you." His warm breath caressed my skin.

Lovingly, he sealed his lips over mine. The taste of him filled my mouth. The feeling of his soft lips against mine felt heavenly. Having my body so close to his felt so perfect, so right.

I pulled my lips away from his and once more stared into his brown eyes, "Maximus, I am with child." I had planned on telling him today and the moment was perfect. I scooted a little bit away from him and grasped him hand and placed it upon my stomach. Pure happiness filled his gaze as he looked upon our hands that were placed upon my belly.

"I am to be a father." He whispered. "We are to be parents."

"I have two names picked out. One for a girl and one for a boy." I spoke softly as I gazed upon my stomach. "Artemis for the boy." I smiled as I spoke that name. The name of my father.

"And for the girl?" Maximus asked curiously.

"Arendella. I must say that I am truly hoping for a girl. But if I were to have a boy I would love him just as much."

Maximus smiled that beautiful smile of his that I've come to love so much. His hand rubbed my stomach carefully and lovingly. "I cannot wait to meet our little gift from the gods."

Today was truly perfect. Nothing could ruin it.

Suddenly a cloaked man stepped out of the forest and advanced toward us. As he approached something in my head screamed danger. Quickly Maximus and I jumped to our feet. The stranger stood at the end of the red blanket and lowered his hood. A man with pale skin and crimson hair stood before us. His red eyes gazing upon us. Something was off about this man, something was wrong with him. I gripped Maximus's arm.

"What do you want?" Maximus demanded as he stood in front of me.

"My name is Andakile. The new king of Raz'noak."

"That kingdom has been in ruin for years." I said to him.

"Was. I have revived it with the help of the seal."

My stomach sank. Had this man really destroyed one of the seals? If so, then this meant his visit here would mean he was seeking to destroy Theleshara's seal as well. I tugged on the sleeve of Maximus's tunic. We needed to leave. Now.

"I must ask you to leave, now." My husband demanded.

Andakile merrily chuckled at Maximus's demand. His hand slid down and rested upon the pommel of his sheathed sword. Panic surged through my being. We had not brought our staffs. We were weaponless.

"Lyanthian, go back to Theleshara. Now."

"No. I refuse to leave your side."

"Yes, do stay. It'll be a lot more interesting." The sword hissed as it was drawn forth from its sheath.

Maximus shoved me behind him, guarding me with his body. Fear dwelled inside me. Clawing at me. I prayed to the gods that they would keep my husband safe. That nothing bad would befall upon him.

"This can go two ways; One being that you simply tell me where the seal is hidden and I shall let you live. Two being that I slowly kill one of you while I force the other to watch until you tell me where it is." He glanced at us with a malicious smirk written upon his face. "So which one shall it be?"

"Neither." Maximus said.

"Tsk. Tsk." Andakile shook his head from side to side. "I guess it shall be two then."

Everything happened so quickly it seemed like a blur. Maximus shoved me to the ground as Andakile's sword sliced through his shoulder and into his chest, nearly cutting his body in half. Warm blood sprayed across my face as my husband fell to the ground in front of me. His brown lifeless eyes stared into mine. I was frozen in shock. Was my husband really dead? Could this be a dream? Then the man marched toward me. He stood over my body, looking down upon me.

"I can smell another life growing inside of you."

His voice sent a chill down my spine. My body was shaking in fear.

"Tell me where the seal is or I kill your unborn child."

My eyes glanced over at my lover's lifeless body. He gave up his life to protect mine and our child's. And to protect the seal. My heart beat crazily within my chest.

What should I do?

Save my child and give this man the location of the seal?

Or save the seal and lose my child?

My hand rested upon my stomach. My child was in there. Maximus's child was growing inside of me. Our child. Tears burned within my eyes. I knew the right thing to do. The seal was more important. I had to protect my people. All of Lylanalian. That is my role as queen. And this was the sacrifice that I had to make.

I'm so sorry my child.

I'm so sorry Maximus.

My eyes met with Andakile's crimson gaze. He shook his head, thinking of me as a fool.

Suddenly, his foot slammed into my stomach. The force of his kick knocked the breath out of me. Pain crippled my being. I felt a warmness between my thighs. I glanced down to see blood coating my white dress in red. My pelvic area felt as though something were being ripped from it. Blood oozed onto the sandy beach. Tears stained my cheeks as they rushed from my eyes like a waterfall. The pain was too great, the force of his kick was too much. Bile rose in my throat and escaped my mouth. Stomach fluids and blood gushed from my mouth. I retched until my throat my burned.

The man knelt before me. "*If only you had told me where the seal was, your husband and your child would still be alive.*" His lips brushed against my ear, "*Their deaths are on your shoulders.*" With that he stood to leave. Disappearing into the forest.

My eyes wondered over to my husband's body. I reached out a shaking hand and held his cold hand in mine. My other hand gripped over my stomach. My two loves were gone. Taken from me. My heart shattered. Tears streamed down my face. My cries of sorrow echoed within my ears. I had prayed to the gods to protect my lover. Why hadn't they done so? Why did they allow that man to murder him and my unborn child? Why were the gods being so cruel?

I don't know how long I had been laying there but I was awoken by a familiar voice. When I opened my eyes I was met with the face of my closest friend. Her white hair was all that I could make out with my blurry vision.

"*Lyanthian can you hear me?*" Her panicked voice shook with concern and sadness.

Her sapphire eyes glided down my body and saw the source of all the blood. Her hand clasped over her mouth as a gasp escaped her. "*You were with child?*" She choked back her tears as she eyed my husband's lifeless body.

"*I couldn't imagine the pain you must be feeling now, Lyanthian. I wish there were something I could do to relieve you of this pain.*" Tears swelled within her eyes and cascaded down her rosy, freckled cheeks.

"*Alleonna, promise to me that one day when you are with child again and the baby is born a girl that you shall name her Arendella. That would make me truly happy.*" I gazed upon her stomach and rested my hand upon it. Though the gods have decided that having a child was not meant for me, I still wished for an Arendella to be born into this world.

*   *   *   *

I felt as though I had just relived that day all over again. The memory was so strong. The pain I felt on that day brought itself upon me once more. Without realizing it my hand was clasped over my stomach. My child lived and died within me, never seeing the light of day. Never getting to see its father or mother. The child had done nothing to deserve death.

"Do you take pride in making people suffer? Do you take pride in taking the lives of innocents? Of children?" Anger flared throughout my body like an inferno.

"I do what I deem necessary. If I must kill unborn children or born children to get what I want, then so be it. Their lives mean nothing to me." His voice was so cold. This man truly had no heart.

"If you think forcing me to relive painful memories will weaken me you are wrong. They only strengthen me and remind me that you must be brought down."

"Ah, that's a shame. That trick works on *your* Arendella." He chuckled. "Or the Arendella that you wish was your blood daughter."

"You stay away from her!" Once more I shot a beam of magic toward him. My hatred and anger for the king fueled my power.

His sword easily sliced through my magic, the beam split in two and shot right by him. I couldn't fight him with just magic. I had to rely on physical strength as well. My hand rested upon the pommel of my sword that was strapped to my belt. It was ready for battle whenever I needed it.

"I haven't gotten a chance to use my true power. You might be a worthy opponent." Andakile popped his neck and re-enforced his grip on his sword.

He raised it into the sky and slashed it through the empty air. A crimson pulsating force of magic was sent my way. It charged at me, crackling and popping. I summoned forth a protective dome that draped around me. His magic smashed into the dome. The force of the hit shook the earth beneath me and sent cracks running throughout my barrier.

I couldn't just rely on barriers and protective magic. I needed to attack. But he was too strong, my magic was hardly a match against his. A strategy formed within my mind. Multiple projectile magical attacks would prove useful. If I could distract him long enough I could gain the upper hand and take him down.

"Islandia o'thara!" I summoned my magic forth.

The ruby upon my staff glowed brightly as icicle shards formed within the air. Hundreds of them floated before me and with a slash of my staff they hurtled toward the king. Andakile sliced through my icicle shards, but not all of them. Some landed a hit. Embedding themselves into his skin. Tar trickled from the wounds.

I didn't give him the chance to ready himself for another string of attacks. *"Camela o'fenier!"*

Orbs of flames raced through the air, the fiery spheres igniting the dark night in an orange glow. Then they halted and floated within the air, surrounding the king in a ring of inferno. His crimson gaze locked with mine as the orbs of fire attacked him all at once. Each of them slamming into his cursed body. His body was in flames but… he just stood there. Doing nothing while fire ate away at him. Then menacing chuckles echoed from him. Seeming as though a thousand evil laughing voices cackled through the night. He slowly marched forth. A malicious smile spread wide across his face exposing his sharpened teeth. He stood just a few feet away from me, spreading his arms out wide. There was a shift in the air and the fire surrounding his body began to grow more intense, their light growing brighter. Then the fiery inferno that was incasing his body lifted into the air, removing itself from his being. It surrounded him in a fiery aura. Then the fire gathered together behind him, forming a massive fiery whirlwind. Andakile clapped his hands together and targeted the fire at me. My vision focused upon the massive inferno, the flames crackled and hissed through the air as it charged toward me.

Acting quickly I summoned upon my magic and my body took flight into the night sky, missing the king's attack by mere inches. The flames grazed the bottom of my shoes as they sizzled beneath me. The king's glowing crimson gaze locked upon me, watching my hovering body. Soon a red mist crawled over his body, creating a red aura pulsating off his being. Then, his feet lifted from the ground and slowly he met with me in the sky. His cursed sword dangled in his grasp. His eyes fixed upon me with an intent to defeat me. Written in his gaze was murder. No more would he play easy, now he would use his power to its fullest.

"It's time to end this, Lyanthian." He gripped his sword with both hands.

"It is, Andakile." I held my staff before me.

Silence draped around us. A chilling breeze swept over our hovering bodies. Our gazes never broke from each-other, we were locked in one another's eyes. His brow knitted together as his reptilian tongue flickered from between his cracked lips. A cold sweat crawled down my spine. My hands firmly grasped my staff, my knuckles turning white.

The fiery aura surrounding his body intensified as he summoned forth his magic. The aura then formed into eight tentacles. They swayed in the air behind him, waving from side to side slowly. A series of words escaped my lips as I chanted and called forth my power. Water formed within the air around my body, taking on the form of tentacles as well. Andakile raised an eyebrow and smirked. Suddenly, his magic thundered toward me. His tentacles crawled through the air, racing one another in a competition to reach my being. As his magic grew closer I sent my own tentacles to meet with his. The two forms of magic slammed into one another. A rush of wind blew my way as our magic collided.

One of my hands slipped from my staff and found its way to the pommel of my sword that rested upon my hip. The sword that my father bestowed upon me many years ago. My hand gripped around the hilt. Lowering my staff to my side, but still holding onto the magic I had called forth for the tentacles, I held the sword before me. Closing my eyes, I took a deep breath, settling my thoughts, erasing my doubts and worries. Opening my eyes once more I was filled with new found determination. My body shot forward, my sword sliced through my waves of magic, through the king's magic. A warrior's yell rose in my throat and escaped my lips. Andakile's eyes grew in amazement, his brows rose in surprise. Quickly he called back his magic and rose his sword to block mine. Our swords collided against one another, the sound of steel striking steel rang within my eardrums.

Slipping my staff through a notch on my belt I gripped the sword's hilt with my other hand. Our swords fought against one another, Andakile and I's faces grew close to each other. His crimson eyes glowed with hatred. His breath reeked causing my nostrils to snarl. I thrust my sword against his, pushing my body away from him. We circled each other in the sky, readying ourselves for an attack.

In an attempt to taunt me, Andakile brought his sword to his face, his reptilian tongue slid from his mouth and trailed down the steel sword. Tar trickled from his tongue and down the steel, coating it in a black sticky mass. Though the sight did sicken me I refused to let him taunt me.

"Enough of these childish games, Andakile!"

As I shouted, my body soared through the air. I slashed my sword down upon the king when I was close enough to do so. He raised his sword and blocked my attack. While my attention was focused else where my eyes caught the glint of steel, the king had taken a dagger from his belt and was aiming to stab me with it. Everything slowed around me. Slowly the sharpened end of the dagger inched toward my ribs. A malicious, toothy smile, spread across the king's lips as his gaze was written in a crazed thirst for blood.

I knew I had to evade this attack but if I moved then the king's sword would slice through my chest. There was nothing I could do. I repositioned my body as the dagger embedded itself into my lower ribs. I gasped out in pain. The steel slid into my skin like it were softened butter. A warm liquid trickled down my side, cascading down my legs, and falling like rain drops from my feet. My blood dripped down through the sky like red rain. The king withdrew his sword and floated back away from me. My sword slipped through my grasp as my hand gripped my side.

Then, I was falling. Plummeting through the air. The ground was growing closer and closer. The king's crimson gaze locked upon my falling body, a smirk forming upon his lips. Then his gaze glided toward the fountain, the final seal. He began to hover toward it.

No. I refused to let him win. My shaking hand removed my staff from a notch on my belt, then my lips whispered an incantation. Suddenly, my body stopped falling. Once more I hovered within the air with the help of magic. Pain surged through my being. Blood oozed from my wound. My hand gripped my side. I didn't have the time to heal myself, I had to stop the king. Quickly I raced toward him, his focus was upon the fountain. My body slammed into his broad back. A howl of surprise escaped him as we plummeted to the ground tangled together. My arms wrapped themselves around his neck, his long nails dug into my skin as he tried to free himself from my grasp. His elbow smashed into my ribs, into my wound. A scream of agony rose in my throat and echoed throughout the night. Though pain rang out through my being my grasp on the king never weakened. If I were going to die this way, then he shall too.

Down, down, down we fell.

The ground below us was growing ever closer with each passing second. Soon we would crash into the earth. Soon we would both be dead. I closed my eyes, bracing myself for the impact. In the darkness of my vision flickered the faces of the people who I loved. Arendella's smiling face appeared first and faded away, next was Queen Titiana. Many more faces appeared before me. But the last face to manifest within in my mind was my lover. Maximus. Within his arms he held a baby wrapped in a pink blanket. He smiled brightly, reaching his hand toward to me, he beckoned for me to join him in the heavens.

Soon my love.

A burning sensation enveloped my arms. I opened my eyes to see a fiery aura forming upon the king's body. A crimson shield circled around us. My gaze wondered down to the ground. It was close, too close. Then we slammed into the hard earth, the impact rattling the bones in my body, causing my vision to blacken. My arms slipped away from Andakile's neck.

A groan escaped him as he stood, "Now it's time for me to destroy this seal and conquer the land of Lylanalian." He spat at me as he advanced toward the fountain, gripping his sword.

I forced myself to stand though my body protested heavily. My bones ached. My ribs wept with crimson. But I refused to lose. I refused to fail my people. I reached out for my staff and planted the dagger end of it into the dirt ground. The earth rippled beneath me as I whispered an incantation. Vines erupted from the earth and raced along the ground toward the king. They snaked around his ankles and wrapped themselves around his legs. He fell with a heavy thud, the vines encased his body, wrapping around him until only his head was showing.

I removed my staff from the earth and walked toward the king. I pointed the dagger end of my staff toward his throat. "It is over, Andakile. You have lost."

A chuckled escaped him, turning into a crazed laugh. He howled like a mad man. The vines that were wrapped around his body began to shrivel and die. No longer were they green but a dark brown color. He moved his arms and the vines cracked and fell away from his body like dry leaves.

"I am afraid you are mistaken, Lyanthian. For you see, I have won and you have lost."

He held out his hand before him, exposing his palm. Crimson lighting sparked between his fingers and crackled down to his palm, forming a crimson sphere. It grew and grew until it was bigger than his hand. Then the sphere shot forth, pulsating through the air, lighting sparking from it as it raced toward me. Quickly I called forth a protective dome. It draped around me but the king's magic blasted through my barrier and slammed into my being. His dark magic exploded around me. My body flew through the air and landed hard upon the ground. As I tried to stand thorny vines burst forth from the ground, tangling around my arms and legs. When I moved, the vines tightened around me causing their thorns to sink into my skin, crimson droplets began to bead down my arms and legs.

Andakile peered over his shoulder and smirked. Turning his gaze away from me he focused upon the fountain that stood before him. He raised his cursed sword above his head, a fiery aura radiated from the steel.

"No!" A yell escaped me as I tried desperately to break free from the king's magic. The thorns dug deeper into my skin, blood wept from my wounds.

His sword came slashing down toward the fountain. The blade bit through the stone, slicing the top portion of the fountain off. A blue light flooded from inside the structure and slowly the symbol rose into the air. Its blue light ignited the dark night. Andakile stood before the floating symbol. His sword dangled from his grasp. His crimson eyes glided up and down the symbol. "Finally, I'll be unstoppable."

Saying that, he once again raised his sword over his head and brought it down upon the symbol. The steel sliced through it. A red light exploded from the destroyed seal and black clouds spilled out onto the land and crawled toward Andakile. The black mist circled at his feet and made its way up to his chest. Two thin crimson light beams emerged from the seal and snaked through the air toward him. They hovered in the air before his face and then they shot into his eyes. A roar escaped him and bellowed throughout the night. Andakile's body rose into the sky, the black clouds whirled around his being like a tornado. Crimson lightning sparked and flew into the night sky, thunder roared overhead.

I couldn't believe what my eyes were seeing. The clouds dispersed revealing the king. His skin was now fully grey, his long crimson hair whirled around him, those red eyes of his glowed brightly in the dark of the night, he had grown in height, his arms and chest were more muscular. Then a pair of black smoke wings spread out behind him. Dark wisps floated along the edges of the wings. His armor was painted in black with intricate red designs that danced along the darkened metal.

He glanced down toward his hands, they were engulfed in a fiery aura. Andakile tilted his head back to glance at the sky and then beams of red shot from his hands into the dark sky. Black clouds formed, powerful winds shook the trees around us causing them to bend backward. The temperature dropped drastically. Rain began to pour down crazily like a waterfall. Lightning lit up the red sky as it crackled through the dark clouds.

The king lowered from the sky, waltzed toward me, and knelt to the ground before my trapped body. His fingers traced down my blood stained arm. He stared at the crimson liquid that coated his grey hand, then his tongue slid out of his mouth and licked at the substance. There was no emotion in his gaze, nothing.

He stood, "Now I am the true ruler." His crimson eyes gave me a once over. "I shall not kill you. You are of no threat to me." The corner of his mouth turned in disgust. With a wave of his hand the vines released their hold on me.

"Mark my words, Andakile. There shall be one person strong enough to bring you down. Do not sleep so soundly at night."

His nostrils snarled, "You think that anyone shall be foolish enough to stand against me? Everyone shall hide away in fear while I conquer this land. And for anyone that is naïve enough to fight me, then I shall end their pathetic lives, slowly." He turned his back to me and began to walk away but stopped suddenly in his tracks. "Mark *my* words, Lyanthian. I shall kill everyone that you love, just like I did with your lover and child."

King Andakile marched into the dark night, a mass of black clouds swept down from the sky and covered his being. He vanished, carried away by the dark mist. I peered around me, my eyes landing upon the sight of the demolished fountain. My fingers dug into the muddy earth as I crawled my way toward the remains of the last seal. My side throbbed in pain as I urged my body forward. Rain pelted down from the heavens. Thunder rolled overhead, shaking the ground beneath me. I raised myself from the ground and sat before the destroyed fountain. I peered down at my body, mud covered my clothing. Tiny wounds freckled my arms and legs. A massive crimson spot stained my golden gown. My eyes wondered along the ground and they landed upon a piece of marble that was once part of the beautiful fountain.

Many emotions boiled inside of me at once; failure, lose, frustration. I pounded my fists on the muddy ground as a cry escaped me.

I had failed Theleshara and my people.

Failed the land of Lylanalian.

Failed as a queen.

And now everyone shall suffer because I had failed to protect the seal.

The story continues in book three...

To: Jeff

From: Brianna
Paige
McClendon

Hope you enjoy!

Made in the USA
Lexington, KY
30 April 2016